W9-CPN-985

WHILE THE CLOCK TICKED

HARDY BOYS MYSTERY STORIES

"Mr. Wandy!" Joe shouted. "Wait!
I'll help you. Don't move."

Hardy Boys Mystery Stories

WHILE THE CLOCK TICKED

BY

FRANKLIN W. DIXON

NEW YORK
GROSSET & DUNLAP
Publishers

In this new story, based on the original of
the same title, Mr. Dixon has incorporated
the most up-to-date methods used by police
and private detectives.

ISBN: 0-448-08911-4 (TRADE EDITION)

ISBN: 0-448-18911-9 (LIBRARY EDITION)

CONTENTS

WHILE THE CLOCK TICKED

CHAPTER I

A Mysterious Tip

"I WONDER who that man is, Frank," whispered blond Joe Hardy, peering curiously from a second-floor window of their home. "He looks worried."

His brother glanced down at the stranger just departing from the front door. "Let's ask Aunt Gertrude. She talked with him."

Joe, a year younger and more impetuous than his eighteen-year-old, dark-haired brother, bounded downstairs. Frank followed.

"Aunt Gertrude," Joe cried excitedly, "who was the man who just left?"

Fenton Hardy's sister shrugged. "I don't know," said the tall, black-haired woman. "He wanted your father to solve a mystery. I told him Fenton was away."

The boys waited to hear no more. As they

dashed out the door, Frank said, "Why, Auntie, we're detectives too, remember?"

Joe was first to reach the stranger, who was about to drive off in a convertible. "Sir," he said earnestly, "please wait!"

As Frank caught up with his brother, the tall, vigorous-looking man stared at them through rimless glasses. The boys saw a wary look come over his face. "Well, what is it?" he demanded impatiently.

Quickly Frank explained. "We're Frank and Joe Hardy. Our aunt told us you wanted Dad to solve a mystery. Since he isn't at home, we thought maybe we could help you."

"Mr. Hardy's sons!" the man burst out. "Listen! I'm in real trouble, and I must see your father. I'll pay any amount to contact him. Just tell me where he can be reached."

Joe shook his head. "No use, Mr.—?"

"Dalrymple. Raymond Dalrymple of Lakeside. I'm in the banking business. Look here, why *can't* I get in touch with Fenton Hardy?"

"Dad and Mother have gone on a camping trip up in Maine. They can't be reached by telephone or telegraph."

A look of desperation came into the banker's eyes. "I can't entrust this business to boys," he muttered, as if thinking aloud.

"It's not as if we were beginners at sleuthing," Joe said persuasively. "Frank and I have helped

Dad on many cases." He gave a sudden grin. "Even Aunt Gertrude would admit we've had some success, too."

Mr. Dalrymple smiled faintly, then gave the boys a swift, penetrating look. "Like to follow in your world-famous dad's footsteps, eh—be detectives yourselves, would you?" His keen eyes took in the hiking boots and khaki outfits they wore. "Fine summer morning for a hike." He added abruptly, "Which direction are you taking?"

Before either boy could answer he went on:

"Try Shore Road, past the harbor. Turn off and follow Willow River Road out into the country."

"Why?" Frank queried, intrigued.

"You'll pass the old Purdy place. Know the one I mean?"

"Big stone house," Joe answered. "Slate roof. Stands back from the road a way. Nobody's been living there for some time, though."

"You're observant," the banker commented. For a moment he was silent, as if trying to make a decision. He pulled nervously at his hatbrim. "Okay, boys," he said finally. "You want to be detectives. Take a look around there on your hike."

The brothers waited expectantly for further explanation. But instead of giving any, the banker started his car and drove off.

"Boy, oh boy!" Joe exploded. "We have a mystery, and we don't know what it's about!"

Frank, too, was baffled. "Well, let's get back to the house. The fellows will be here soon."

The Hardys found Aunt Gertrude waiting for them in the living room. "Well, I suppose you're head over heels in another case. I can tell by your faces. What *did* that man want?"

Frank and Joe gave her a quick report. "We didn't find out why he wanted to see Dad," Frank admitted. "But one thing's certain. We'll hike right to the Purdy place."

Miss Hardy cast her eyes upward. "Well, if you're bound to get yourselves involved in another risky case, I should know there's no stopping you until you solve it!"

The boys exchanged knowing winks. Beneath her peppery manner, their aunt was actually very proud of her nephews' sleuthing abilities.

Suddenly there came a loud banging from the back of the house and a *clomp, clomp* of heavy footsteps through the kitchen. The next moment a chunky, jolly-looking boy marched into the living room. He had a knapsack on his back, and wore big high-top boots.

"Ready?" he sang out. "Tramp, tramp, the boys are marching! I got the provisions, so don't worry."

"My only worry is, Chet, that you'll eat 'em before the rest of us have a chance." Joe laughed. Chet Morton was one of the Hardys' best friends.

"Decided where you want to go?" inquired Biff

Hooper, another chum, who had come in behind Chet.

"Let's try Willow River Road," Joe suggested offhandedly.

"Suits me," lanky Biff agreed readily.

With a hasty farewell to Aunt Gertrude, the four pals set out. Brisk walking brought them swiftly out of town on the Shore Road, which followed horseshoe-shaped Barmet Bay. Looking back, they could see the docks of the harbor.

Some distance ahead of them was the bridge which spanned the mouth of Willow River where it emptied into the bay. The boys turned right down the river road, which had deep ditches on both sides. They rounded the sharp corner Indian file, Frank leading, then crossed to the left-hand side of the road so they would be facing any oncoming traffic.

Suddenly there was a screeching of tires behind them. The hikers whirled to see the gleaming chromium grille of a black limousine. The big car had swerved wide around the turn, hugging the left shoulder of the road.

"Jump!" shouted Frank. He shoved Chet Morton into the ditch and landed on top of him. Joe and Biff dived to the side also.

Even in the instant of leaping to safety, Joe had taken a penetrating glance at the driver of the car. Now, as the boys picked themselves up, he was able to report.

"Mean-looking customer—husky, with a big jaw. Close crew cut."

"Well, he nearly flattened us!" complained Biff. "What's a tough guy like that doing in a limousine?"

"Running down innocent hikers," Chet answered indignantly.

They climbed back to the road, and started out

once more. Presently they came to a section of large houses, set back on extensive grounds. Some of the estates were well kept, but a few had fallen into disrepair. Those on the left, the boys knew, were bounded in the rear by Willow River.

Half an hour later, as they rounded a sharp bend, a long, high stone wall came into view. A tangle of ivy clung to the stones, and close-growing young trees partially screened the wall from the road. Here and there, however, the boys caught a glimpse of a bluish slate roof.

"The Purdy house," said Joe, looking with intent curiosity.

"Gone to seed, since the old man died," Biff Hooper added. "I hear he was a queer fellow."

Something in Joe's lingering tone had warned the easygoing Chet Morton that there was an underlying significance to the remark.

"Wait a minute, fellows," he began. "Something tells me we didn't come this way just by accident. If it's another mystery, you can count me out! I'm not over the last one yet!"

"Well, to be honest, Chet," Frank said with a chuckle, "we did have a visitor, just before you showed up. He suggested we look over this place."

"No fooling!" Biff exclaimed eagerly.

The boys had reached the main gate to the place. To their surprise, they found it open, with the marks of automobile tires in the driveway.

As the four walked up the drive, which was lined with the dense green foliage of thick bushes and trees, the silence was broken by a gruff voice:

"Hey, you fellows!"

A figure in the white helmet and black boots of a motorcycle patrolman strode toward them.

"It's Mike DiSalvo," said Joe, recognizing the officer. "What's up, Mike?" The Hardy boys, through their father's detective work and their own, knew all the Bayport policemen.

"Harbor thieves," said the officer briefly. "I was driving up Willow River Road when I spotted them roaring toward me. Then they hit that sharp bend, and I lost sight of them. I was sure they'd ducked in here, but I can't find the car. It was a big, black limousine."

CHAPTER II

Puzzling Clues

"A BLACK limousine! One nearly killed us half an hour ago, Mike!" Frank exclaimed.

As they walked on to the high, rambling gray stone house, Joe gave a description of the tough-looking driver. Mike DiSalvo nodded thoughtfully.

"Sounds like one of the gang," he agreed. "They've been stealing goods from the ships and warehouses for months. We suspected they'd been using that black car, but today was the first time I had a chance at them. Well, that limousine is hot *now!*"

The officer straddled his motorcycle, which stood before the entrance of the old mansion. There was a deafening roar as he started the motor.

"Thanks for the tip, boys!" Mike shouted. "By the way, what are you doing out here?"

"Hike!" shouted Frank in reply.

"Case?" the policeman guessed, grinning.

"Maybe. Know anything about this place?"

The officer throttled down. "Not much, except it's been closed for years. Peculiar that gate being open, though. I *still* think I saw the limousine duck in here. Couldn't be, I guess, since the car is nowhere around."

As the motorcycle rumbled out the driveway, Frank called, "We'll close the gate!"

The roar of the motorcycle died away, and the boys were left in the brooding silence of the run-down, neglected estate.

"Funny," commented Biff Hooper, looking around him. "I never heard of anything mysterious about this place. It's not even supposed to be haunted."

"Well, let's have a look around," Frank suggested. "Mr. Dalrymple acted as though something funny might be going on out here."

"You *do* have a case then!" declared Biff.

"Not exactly," Joe admitted wryly. "I have a hunch that since he couldn't see Dad, Mr. Dalrymple is testing us. He doesn't really expect us to turn up anything."

"He doesn't!" Biff echoed incredulously. "Doesn't he read the newspapers?"

Frank and Joe, though still in high school, had already earned a name for themselves as sleuths. They had been trained by their father, who had been a crack detective in the New York City Police Department. After retiring to go into private practice in the city of Bayport, Fenton Hardy had enhanced his reputation by handling difficult and dangerous cases for the government, large corporations, and private individuals.

From him Frank and Joe had learned the need for careful observation and the importance of laboratory work. In fact, they already had a small but well-equipped lab of their own in the loft above the Hardy garage.

The Tower Treasure, the first mystery the brothers had solved on their own, was one that had puzzled all Bayport and baffled the police. As Fenton Hardy became busier, he allowed his sons to help on his cases. But they worked best on their own, following their own clues and meeting dangers resourcefully. Recently, the young sleuths had encountered several harrowing adventures before they rounded up a gang of jewel thieves in *What Happened at Midnight.*

Frank shrugged. "I guess Joe and I will just have to prove ourselves to Mr. Dalrymple."

"Right. Let's get started," Joe urged. "How about Biff and me checking doors and windows?"

Frank agreed. "Meantime, Chet and I will look over the grounds."

The boys separated. Frank and Chet, examining the earth carefully, moved around the big house until they came to the back.

"Whoops!" Frank exclaimed suddenly, bending down.

"What? I don't see anything," Chet said. "Just matted grass!"

Frank pushed aside the limp blades and pointed out the distinct impression of a footprint in the earth.

"Somebody came through here last night," he said. "The grass was flattened and broken when it was dewy."

"Pal, you sure have X-ray eyes," Chet marveled.

By tracking carefully, Frank followed the prints down the yard and into a belt of thick woods where a path, apparently a well-used trail, led to Willow River.

"Whoever was here probably came to do some fishing," Chet remarked.

"Could be," Frank murmured. To himself he added, "Or the person might have been after something besides fish."

Presently the four boys met once more.

"Find anything?" Frank asked his brother.

"All the doors and windows seem to be locked," he replied. "But there are scratches around the front-door lock. Somebody must have tried to open it in the darkness."

Briefly, Frank described his own findings. "Doesn't add up to much," he admitted. "Not enough to impress Mr. Dalrymple."

"Well, thank goodness!" declared Chet.

"That's one mystery we're rid of! Now let's do what we started out to do."

"Chet means let's eat." Biff grinned.

But Joe stood silent, looking up at the rambling stone house. "It's such a big old place," he mused. "For all we know, somebody could be inside it right now, watching every move we make."

"Yes," Frank agreed. "I wouldn't write off the footprints and key scratches. Take them together, with Mr. Dalrymple's queer hint—I'll bet they do mean something."

Chet cast an uneasy glance at the blank dark windows above his head. "Let's go! Are we hiking, or aren't we?"

"So good for your appetite," Biff teased.

"Okay, okay. I just don't like the idea of something peeking at me out of windows," the stout boy blurted.

Frank grinned. "All right. We'll get away from the spooks."

With his knapsack jiggling up and down, Chet eagerly turned and marched down the driveway to the road. Laughing, the other three boys followed. Secretly, the Hardys felt a strong urge to investigate further, and hoped they would have the chance to do so.

As they left the driveway, Frank closed the heavy wooden gate behind them. But there was no way for him to lock it, since he did not have the key. Soon the four friends again reached the sunshine of Willow River Road and resumed their hike.

"I don't understand why a sensible banker like Mr. Dalrymple would be interested in a run-down place like that," said Joe.

"Forget it!" Chet begged. "Think about something pleasant. Forget mysteries!"

"Concentrate on important things," Biff needled him. "Eating and sleeping, for instance."

"Yes, eating and sleeping." Chet defended himself. "Who can live without food? Luscious, delectable food! And sleep—soothing sleep! We grow when we sleep."

"*You* grow much more, and you'll be a giant beach ball." Biff grinned.

But Chet was now scanning the countryside. The boys had left the estates behind. A heavily wooded hill rose up on their right. A field of fresh-cut, drying hay fell away on the left. At the bottom of the field a huge oak tree spread its shading limbs invitingly.

"Now *there* is the place for both," Chet said. "First our lunch. Then, refreshing sleep—before our walk home."

Frank, Joe, and Biff looked at one another, eyes twinkling. There remained a full hour until lunchtime!

"No," said Biff. "Thumbs down."

"Why?" Chet pleaded.

"No water. What's a picnic without water?"

Another half hour went by. Chet sighted a clear stream, flashing in the sun, pouring through a green meadow. "There!" he exclaimed in triumph.

"Uh-uh!" said Joe, poker-faced. "No shade. I can't eat in the blazing sun. Hurts my digestion."

"Oh-h," the stout boy moaned, but proceeded doggedly ahead. Presently the woods closed in on both sides, and the road crossed a small creek.

"Now?" Chet sighed hopefully.

"No." Frank shook his head.

"Oh-h! *Now* why?"

"Too many trees. No sun. Can't eat without a little sun."

But at last, when Frank, Joe, and Biff had agreed, by a wink at one another, that the proper time for lunch had come, they simply jumped into a ditch at the side of the road. "Chow time!"

"But . . ." Chet stammered. "There's no water!" Biff pointed to a trickle in a culvert nearby.

"Well, there's no shade!" Chet argued. Joe grinningly indicated a tree twenty feet away.

"And under this bank, it's not even really sunny!" Chet pointed out.

"Just right." Frank chuckled and dug into Chet's knapsack.

"Say, cut it out!" Chet bellowed. "I have half a mind not to give you fellows any lunch at all!"

"Ho! Now you want us to starve!" Biff laughed

as he and the Hardys lifted out succulent sandwiches, a jar of home-preserved peaches, a gallon
Thermos of chilled milk, and slabs of chocolate
cake.

"Lucky for you, Chet," Joe teased, "you
brought enough so there's some food left for you."

The heavy-set boy, though pretending indig-
nation, settled down to enjoy his share of the
lunch. Then the Hardys and Biff followed Chet's
example and took a nap after the hearty meal.
"Not a bad idea," Joe murmured as he dozed off.

An hour later, however, the four chums were
hiking back to Bayport.

Once in town, Frank and Joe said good-by as
Chet and Biff went off toward their own homes.
When the brothers reached home, they were met
at the door by Aunt Gertrude.

"About time!" she greeted them impatiently.
"Get in here, quick!"

Bewildered, the boys followed her into the living room. To their astonishment, Mr. Raymond
Dalrymple was pacing back and forth in front of
the fireplace.

The tall man wheeled as they entered. "You
boys still want to handle my case for me?" he demanded gruffly. "Well, it's yours!"

CHAPTER III

Grim Warnings

"I ASKED people about you," the banker said as the startled Hardy boys took seats. "Mind you, I wouldn't have done that if I weren't desperate. You looked like a pair of inexperienced kids to me."

"And what did you find out, Mr. Dalrymple?" Joe asked politely.

"That you really have done some fine work on problems like mine. In fact, the police here told me that if Fenton Hardy were out of town, I couldn't do better than to call in his sons."

Although Frank and Joe were proud to hear this, both remained quiet and attentive.

"You say nothing," Mr. Dalrymple noted. "Good. I like that. Now, to business. Did you stop at the Purdy estate on your walk today?"

"Yes," Frank answered.

"Well—notice anything?" Dalrymple eyed him narrowly.

"When we got there," Frank explained, "the gate was open. A motorcycle policeman looking for harbor thieves was in the driveway. After he left we found some footprints—"

"Footprints?" Mr. Dalrymple interrupted, suddenly very agitated. "When were they made?"

"Sometime in the night, after the dew fell."

"But the gate!" the banker broke in. "I locked that gate when I left the place last night!"

At this the boys sat bolt upright with surprise. "You were out there, sir?" Joe burst out.

"Of course. I own the house."

"You!" Joe exclaimed.

"Yes. I was out there yesterday until shortly before dark. Now, from what you tell me, someone else was there later—perhaps to injure me!"

"Wait a minute!" Frank said. "Why don't you tell us your whole story, Mr. Dalrymple?"

"Right. You're absolutely right," the banker agreed, regaining his composure. After a moment's thought, he began:

"Mr. Jason Purdy was a wealthy and eccentric man, as you no doubt know. His estate was left to the Bayport Library. I recently purchased the house and grounds on speculation—hoping to sell them later at a higher price. However, when I inspected the house, I discovered a strange thing!"

Frank, Joe, and Aunt Gertrude leaned forward excitedly. "What?" Joe pressed.

"A secret room on the second floor," the man replied. As the boys listened intently he went on, "It was built right into the middle of the house. When Mr. Purdy inherited the property, he had the hidden chamber fixed up like a bank vault, fireproof, with insulated walls and no windows. Air is provided by hidden ventilators. The only door is made of heavy steel, and is closed with a time lock."

"But why would Mr. Purdy have wanted a room like that?" asked Joe in amazement.

"He was eccentric, remember?" Mr. Dalrymple smiled. "He didn't trust banks. He kept all his valuables in the secret room. He used it as a kind of retreat, too. I looked for any hoard of valuables that might be hidden there, but found none. Purdy's servant, who knew of the room, had faithfully turned over everything to the executors.

"Well," the Hardys' visitor confided, "I did not plan to live in the house, or use the other rooms, but I liked the hidden retreat. Many times I have to handle propositions that demand close figuring and solitary work. As soon as I discovered that secret room, I realized it would make an ideal private office. So I decided to use it.

"I moved in a small table, a typewriter, and my private files. When I left the room, I would set the time lock, and then no one, not even myself, could get in until the appointed hour."

"Of course," Frank agreed. "That's the principle of a time lock."

The banker looked at him sharply. "What would you say if I told you that this room has been entered several times—*in my absence?*"

"Is the lock reliable?" Joe questioned.

"I'm sure of it! I know these locks."

"I'd say," Frank deduced, "that you couldn't have expected us to find out much about a secret room in a house we couldn't enter."

Mr. Dalrymple nodded his approval. "I see you've earned your reputation. I'll have duplicate door and gate keys made for you." He looked somber. "You see, there have been threats to my life!"

"Where? How?" Joe cried, springing up.

In grim silence, Mr. Dalrymple removed two small, carefully folded sheets of paper from his wallet and handed one to each boy. Joe opened his first. Written in pencil was a warning:

"You must leave this house forever or death will overtake you."

Frank, with a puzzled expression, read the other threat:

"Death while the clock ticks!"

He looked up. "What does this mean?"

"That," replied Mr. Dalrymple somberly, "is what I need a good detective—like your father— to find out. But there is one further point.

Where do you suppose I found those messages?"

"In the secret room with the time lock!" Frank answered promptly.

The visitor gasped. "How did you know?"

"That was the one place which would make the whole mystery a tough one," Frank replied.

"When did you find these notes, Mr. Dalrymple?" asked Joe, undaunted.

"The first one, four days ago. The second, about eight o'clock last night. That's why I came here this morning." Mr. Dalrymple's face paled. "If there *was* a man on the grounds last night, he may have come to kill me!"

Frank frowned. "At any rate, whoever wrote this note seems to know when you're there and when you're not. Could someone with whom you're acquainted be out for revenge?"

"I have no enemies, so far as I know. I have always been scrupulously fair in my dealings."

Joe tried another tack. "There's no other way into this room, Mr. Dalrymple? Have you checked the walls? What else is in it?"

"Nothing but my things, and a fireplace. But the flue is barred, and besides, the chimney is altogether too narrow to admit a man."

Joe suggested that the notes might have been dropped down the chimney. Mr. Dalrymple shook his head. "I found the messages on the rug in the exact center of the room."

"Who else but you knows about the room?"

Frank put in. "Can anyone else but you operate the time lock?"

"I have told no one about the room," the banker retorted somewhat irritably. "So nobody knows of the lock, either! Purdy's servant is dead. It's a fantastic story, but true."

"We certainly want to help you," Frank said. "For safety's sake, why don't you stay away from the house, until you hear from us?"

"All right. I'll let you know when the keys are ready."

After their new client had left, the Hardys discussed the mystery. "He's sincere, I guess," Joe concluded. "But the whole thing doesn't make sense."

"I vote we go out to the Purdy place tonight, at least for another look," his brother said.

Although Aunt Gertrude gloried in her nephews' reputations as detectives, she was inclined to worry a great deal about the boys. Nevertheless, she grudgingly agreed to the proposed expedition.

Darkness found Frank backing the boys' convertible out the Hardy driveway. Five minutes later they had stopped for a traffic light on the main street of Bayport.

Suddenly there was the roar of another engine, a rattle of tin, the raucous bark of an air horn. An old jalopy drew up beside the Hardys.

"Get a load of the fancy machine!" shouted a familiar voice.

The face of Tony Prito, a high school friend, grinned at them. Another pal, Jerry Gilroy, seated at the wheel of the jalopy, added, "Nothing like this old crate."

The brothers grinned back, "Where're you all heading?" Joe asked.

"Party, over at Chet Morton's. Tried to get you. Your line was busy. Come on!" Tony urged.

"Can't," Frank called over.

"What do you mean—can't! What are you fellows up to? Callie, Frank says he can't come!"

Through the back window of the jalopy, Frank caught sight of the sparkling brown eyes and pretty face of his favorite date, Callie Shaw.

"Don't give us that!" Phil Cohen, another friend, stuck his head above the old car's roof on the other side.

"What'll we do?" Frank asked his brother.

"Joe, Iola Morton's expecting you!" Tony shouted coaxingly.

"We'll go," Joe decided. "But we can't stay long."

The two cars drove to the Morton farm, about a mile outside Bayport. Several other cars were parked there already. The Hardys' friends marched the brothers into the house.

"Here they are—the sleuths themselves!" Phil

announced triumphantly, as the group entered a large room filled with young people. "Caught red-handed, trying to make a getaway!"

"What is it, another mystery?" demanded a pretty, blue-eyed girl, coming over to Joe. "You weren't trying to get away from me, were you?" she asked teasingly.

"You know better than that, Iola!" Joe laughed. "May I have this dance?"

The couple swung into a lively step as someone started a record player. Frank danced off with Callie. In a moment the party was in full swing.

About an hour later Frank managed to nudge his brother while dancing. "Move to the French doors, and meet us on the porch," he directed.

"You Hardys are certainly romantic," observed Callie, as the two couples stepped onto the moonlit side porch. "Isn't it a beautiful night?"

"We have to leave—work to do," said Frank. "Honest, Callie and Iola, we hate to go. But we have to. We'll explain when we can."

"You *are* on detective business!" Iola exclaimed. She sighed. "Well, be careful. We'll see you one of these days!"

The brothers said good-by, leaped from the porch, and ran to their car. Soon they had passed through Bayport again and were driving rapidly out along the shore onto Willow River Road.

"Don't look now," Joe said tensely, turning slightly in his seat, "but a car's tailing us!"

CHAPTER IV

Stormy Sleuthing

FRANK glanced in the rear-view mirror at the trailing car, which was some distance behind. "We'll test to find out if he's really after us."

He braked the convertible, slowing quickly. For a moment the strange headlights rushed nearer, then dropped back. The other car *was* keeping the same speed as the Hardys were!

"Okay," said Frank with determination. "We'll settle this right now." Quickly he swung off the road and stopped. The two boys sat watching, with the car top down.

An ordinary-looking sedan rolled toward them. Watching it approach, Joe caught sight of a high aerial at the back.

"Police!" he announced with a surprised laugh. In a moment the brothers were looking into the round, cheerful face of Officer Callahan of the

Bayport Police Department. The officer shook his head in mock disgust.

"I was just saying to Tomlin, here," he remarked, "that's a suspicious car speeding out Willow Road. So it's you Hardys, is it? And us expecting a pair of fleeing harbor thieves!"

"Don't think we're any happier than you are about it," Joe joked in return. "We thought *you* were a couple of crooks following *us*."

"Harbor thieves still busy?" Frank asked. "We met Mike DiSalvo chasing them this morning."

"Busy!" Officer Tomlin exclaimed. "Day and night they're busy, and not a lead on 'em yet, except that big, black car. We're sure they've given up using it now, so we have no lead. For that reason, we're tailing everything we see on this road."

At that moment a large, cream-colored sedan pulled around the unmarked police cruiser and roared into the country.

"Here we go," barked Callahan, as Tomlin pulled away to pursue the car. "Maybe that's the one!"

"Good luck!" the Hardys called.

Frank and Joe now noticed that the moon had been obscured by clouds. The grounds of the nearby estates were completely dark. The air had become hot and sticky.

"It's going to storm," said Frank. "We'd better get going." As though in answer to his remark, there came a faraway rumble.

The boys decided to walk to the Purdy place, since it was only a quarter of a mile away, and they would attract less attention. After switching off their parking lights and putting up the convertible's top, the young detectives walked along the dark road. Soon they came to the high wall of the Purdy estate.

They skirted it until they reached the big wooden gate. It was open.

"Wait!" said Frank in a low voice. "We closed that gate this morning. Somebody's been here since then and might still be around."

"The driveway may be watched," Joe warned. "We'd better find some other way in."

They walked back a distance to a place where the wall was heavily overgrown.

"Shall we climb it?" Joe whispered, testing the vines with a pull.

"No. I had a look at that wall this morning. There are pieces of old jagged, broken glass all along the top. Apparently Jason Purdy didn't like company!"

Frank grasped one of the young trees that had sprung up next to the stone fence. In a moment he had shinned up higher than the wall. The tree bent with Frank's weight, swinging him clear of the dangerous glass. Then Frank dropped to the ground on the other side and the tree snapped back into place.

"Come ahead!" he directed Joe in a whisper.

In a moment Joe was beside Frank, crouching among the bushes along the inside of the wall. The rumble of thunder was closer now. A brief white flicker passed over the black sky, showing the bottoms of thick clouds and the big Purdy mansion off to the left.

Creeping slowly and carefully through the dark brush, no longer daring to talk to each other, the two young sleuths gained the open yard in front of the house. They halted at its edge.

By now the rumble in the sky had given way to cracking, booming thunder. A gusty wind was rushing through the leafy trees over their heads. Flickers of lightning, some bright and some faint, played across the open sky and caused weird, momentary shadows on the walls and roof of the silent mansion. The storm was about to strike.

"Listen!" Frank clutched Joe's arm. "Sounded like someone running."

The brothers strained their hearing to the utmost. Despite the strong wind, the thunder, and the sharp patter of raindrops hitting the leaves like a shower of pebbles, Frank and Joe could hear footsteps. Someone was running, now stepping on a dead branch, now kicking a stone.

A tall man's silhouette crossed the open space in front of the boys and mounted the porch. There a flash of lightning revealed him, bent a little, inserting a key in the lock.

"Dalrymple!" breathed Joe in amazement.

"Are you sure? We warned him to keep away from here! Seems to be having trouble getting in."

The man was turning the key and pulling on the knob. Finally the door opened and he went inside. Expectantly, the boys waited in the rain, which had begun to fall in a heavy rush. To their surprise, the house remained in darkness.

"Why doesn't he turn on a light?" Joe muttered impatiently. "Is he afraid somebody will see it? He said he owned the house. Why should he care?"

"Maybe it isn't Dalrymple."

"Sure looked like him. I got a glimpse of his face. Same build, too. Funny we didn't hear a car coming in. He must have gotten here before we did."

"Well, he must know the place pretty well to move around inside without a light," Frank observed. "Unless," he suggested, "he has gone up to the secret room!"

"Or maybe something's happened to him," Joe said in concern. "The secret room was where he found those threatening messages. The person who wrote the notes might have been there waiting for him!"

Alarmed for the safety of their client, the boys started to make a rush for the house.

But Frank stopped abruptly. "Hold on!" he cautioned. "That man might *not* be Dalrymple.

He could be the person who's been threatening him. This fellow seemed very calm as he went in. You remember how nervous Dalrymple was. Let's wait and see."

"Okay," Joe agreed. "But if it *is* Dalrymple, I'd like to know what his game is."

The boys waited by the edge of the brush while the rain, illuminated by lightning, fell in silver sheets.

"*Sh!*" signaled Joe suddenly. "I heard something. Footsteps again."

As the boys listened they were startled by a light suddenly turned on in a large room with a bay window.

"Come on!" Frank urged. Bending low to avoid being seen, the boys raced across the lawn. The rain pelted their backs, drenching them. In a moment Frank and Joe reached the side of the house and stood under the lighted bay window. Here the Hardys were sheltered from the rain, and invisible to anyone in the room.

Cautiously they moved underneath one of the smaller windows in the bay. Frank made a cradle of his hands. Joe stepped into it with one foot and was hoisted up. Warily, Joe raised his head above the sill.

"What do you see?" Frank hissed.

"A living room—the overstuffed furniture's covered with sheets. Walls are paneled. Big glass chandelier. Nobody's there!"

Warily, Joe raised his head above the sill

"Who turned on the light?"

"Could be the storm caused a temporary power failure, and the current just came back on," Joe surmised.

"Where's Dalrymple or whoever it is we saw? What else is in the room?"

"Big heavy doors—and wow! An enormous grandfather's clock near one corner. Glass front with a swinging brass pendulum. I can hear the clock ticking from here!"

"Ticking?" Frank repeated, shifting under Joe's weight. "A clock ticking in a vacant house!" The same thought flashed through the brothers' minds at once.

"Death while the clock ticks!" was the second threatening message Mr. Dalrymple had received.

"Let me look," Frank said eagerly, and Joe dropped to the ground. They quickly reversed positions.

"I wonder who started the clock and when?" Frank said quietly. "It's the right time," he added, glancing at his wrist watch.

Suddenly, as Frank peered in, the room was plunged into darkness once more. In the same instant the whole house was lit up by a vivid sheet of lightning. A resounding clap of thunder smashed directly overhead. Then an unearthly, bloodcurdling scream rang out from within the mansion!

CHAPTER V

Stolen Treasure

As THE scream died away, footsteps scuttled across the wooden porch. A figure, visible to Frank and Joe in the lightning, leaped into the yard and sprinted down the driveway.

"After him!" shouted Frank, springing to the ground.

But already the fugitive had disappeared between the dark trees bordering the drive. The Hardys heard his heels click on stones, and his heavy breathing. Suddenly Joe tripped in his headlong sprint and went down. Frank doubled his speed. Before he knew it he had run into the fleeing man's back.

"Got you!" he cried, locking his arms about the man's body. Joe came pounding up.

There was a groan of terror from the man. At that instant a streak of lightning made everything bright as day. The boys saw a frightened, familiar face staring at them wildly.

"Mr. Applegate!" the brothers exclaimed.

They could not have been more astonished if the fugitive had been Aunt Gertrude! Their elderly captive was Hurd Applegate, a wealthy collector of art objects and one of Bayport's most eccentric characters. Once Frank and Joe had recovered a valuable stamp collection for him, and he had been their friend ever since.

"The Hardy boys!" Applegate gasped, and went limp with relief in Frank's grasp.

"What are you doing here at this hour of the night, Mr. Applegate?" Joe asked in amazement.

The old man, recovering his strength, lurched forward as though eager to put distance between himself and the Purdy house.

"Oh . . . Frank, Joe . . ." He begged, almost incoherently, "home, get me home . . . it's terrible, awful!" The old man shuddered violently as they supported him down the driveway.

When the three reached the wet, glistening road, he hastened unsteadily across it to his car, parked behind some high bushes. It was a big, old-fashioned automobile. Trembling, he started to open the door.

"Hold on, Mr. Applegate!" Frank commanded. "Can't you tell us what happened? Maybe we can do something about it."

One thing the boys were sure of: Hurd Applegate was not mixed up in anything dishonest. But he was too distraught to do more than stammer over and over his desire to go home.

"Oh! Terrible! Never should have come . . . my jade . . . dreadful. Couldn't just let it go. . . ."

"It's something about his jade collection," said Joe. "But we'll never get a thing out of him at this rate."

"What's more, he's in no shape to drive," Frank said quietly.

"And we should find out about that scream," Joe reminded him. "Mr. Dalrymple *may* be inside—and in trouble."

"I'll go back and investigate," Frank offered. "You drive Mr. Applegate to our house in his car. He's chilled to the bone. Aunt Gertrude will look after him. I'll follow in our car as soon as I can."

The boys helped Mr. Applegate into his car. As Joe started the motor, his brother ran back through the downpour toward the Purdy mansion.

When Frank reached the driveway he saw that the house was dark. He raced to a front window and looked in, but could see nothing. He sounded the big brass door knocker, and when there was no answer, pounded on the door and shouted for Mr. Dalrymple. Frank tried the handle but it was locked. He hurried around to the rear of the house and tried first the back door, then the cellar door, calling continuously. Still there was no response. The house remained dark and silent.

Realizing his efforts were useless, Frank went to his car. The rain had abated and he drove swiftly back to town.

In the meantime, Joe, anxious to get his badly shaken passenger home, chafed at the moderate speed which was the best the old car could do.

When he finally pulled up in front of the Hardys' house he was surprised to find the downstairs brightly lighted. Quickly he assisted Mr. Applegate up the front steps.

"Goodness gracious!" cried Aunt Gertrude, when she opened the door. "Coming home half drowned in the middle of the night!" But at sight of the white, drawn face of the old man, the goodhearted lady changed her tone instantly.

"Here, Joe, bring Mr. Applegate into the kitchen," she ordered crisply. "Luckily I have some hot coffee."

Mr. Applegate was seated in a chair in the cheerfully lighted room. Joe went off for towels and a blanket, while Aunt Gertrude persuaded the elderly man to sip the hot coffee. Mr. Applegate seemed to revive instantly. His eyes cleared. He sat straighter.

"Have to be a regular nurse in a household like this." Miss Hardy smiled. "Where's Frank?" she asked suddenly, but before Joe could answer, she said, "Oh, and here I am, forgetting. There's a man to see you. You go right into the living room. I'll take care of Mr. Applegate."

Surprised, Joe was about to go when the back door opened and Frank entered. Aunt Gertrude whirled to survey her dripping nephew.

"Don't bother to explain," she said wryly. "That man is waiting."

"What happened at the Purdy house?" Joe put in quickly.

"Nothing," Frank replied. "I couldn't get in and got no answer when I called."

"There is a man waiting for you boys in the living room," their aunt interrupted firmly.

Joe beckoned to Frank. Puzzled, they went into the living room. There, turning to greet them, was the tall figure of Raymond Dalrymple!

"Mr. Dalrymple!" gasped Joe. "You're all right!"

"Of course I'm all right!" snapped the banker. "Why shouldn't I be?"

"Well . . . that's good," stammered Frank. "But how did you get here so fast?"

"I don't know what you mean. I didn't get here fast at all. I took my time. I always take my time, even in emergencies."

"We didn't see you leave the Purdy place," Joe blurted out. "And nobody passed me on the way back here."

"Purdy place!" repeated the banker, incredulous. "Why, I've been waiting right here for you two boys an hour and a half." Mr. Dalrymple looked sharply at the brothers' drenched clothes. "Is this your method of handling a case?" he demanded.

"Why, we've just been out on *your* case," Joe retorted heatedly. "We saw someone resembling you go into the Purdy house, which was pitch dark. Then a light went on—and off again. The next instant somebody screamed inside, as though he was being murdered. We were afraid it was you. One man ran out—we caught him. He's right here."

The tall banker looked from Frank to Joe in openmouthed amazement. "I assure you, I haven't been near there. You yourselves told me to stay away."

"You came straight here from Lakeside?" queried Joe.

"Directly from the bank. I was working late."

As the boys exchanged baffled glances, Aunt Gertrude appeared, leading in a considerably stronger Hurd Applegate. The old man's eyes traveled around the room until they rested on Raymond Dalrymple.

"You!" shrieked Hurd Applegate in sudden fury. He leaped across at the astounded banker, who quickly retreated behind a chair. "You, you sneak thief! Give me back my jade! Give it back, I say!"

"Calm yourself, whoever you are," responded the banker with dignity, but obviously angry. "I'm sure I have nothing whatever of yours. Be careful. I'll have the law on you for slander!"

"All my beautiful carvings," Mr. Applegate pleaded, turning to Joe. "Make him give me back my jade figures!"

"I tell you I haven't *got* your infernal jade!" roared Mr. Dalrymple.

"Now, sir," Aunt Gertrude said tartly, "that's enough! Hurd Applegate," she snapped, fixing him with her eye, "sit down and tell your story." Calmed by her tone, the excited man sank meekly into an easy chair and began:

"A fellow I never saw before—looked just like this man—came to my house to examine my rare jade collection. He said he was a dealer and might be able to get me some fine pieces. I was alone in the house."

"Where was Adelia?" asked Aunt Gertrude, referring to the sister who lived with Mr. Applegate.

"Visiting, out of town," he explained. "I showed the man all my figurines, and he asked if I had more. I went into the next room and got my greatest treasure out of the safe, a carved jade chess set, worth a fortune. When I came back in the room, all the figurines were gone and so was he!

"I rushed outdoors and saw him get in a car on the road. Mine was in the drive, so I took after him. I couldn't keep up with the man but I saw him turn down Willow River Road and later into a gate. I parked behind the bushes so he wouldn't spot me. I waited several minutes, then got out and walked right after him."

"That was a risky thing to do," Frank said with a frown.

"I know," Mr. Applegate replied, "but all I could think of was getting back my jade. Well, his car was nowhere in sight, but there was a light in the house. I was scared he'd run if I knocked, so I went around back. The rear door was open, and I went in. I was in a hall. There was a light ahead in one room. I was sneaking up. Then it was pitch black all of a sudden; and right behind me, there was that scream!"

Hurd Applegate trembled violently at the memory. But when Aunt Gertrude eyed him once more, he went on, "I just ran, I didn't know where. I thought *it* was right behind me, going to get me! Then I got caught—by you boys!"

Frank looked at the others. "Well, that clears up a lot. You have a double, Mr. Dalrymple, and *he* stole Mr. Applegate's jade!"

"I don't like it," said the banker, shaking his head. "A double who's a thief."

"This is a case for the police," Frank said, picking up the telephone.

"Do we have to drag my trouble into it?" Mr. Dalrymple asked quickly.

"For now," Frank replied, "we won't mention your case. We'll just report the theft of the jade."

When he hung up he told the others that Chief Collig was going to send men out to search the Purdy house and grounds for the thief.

A few minutes later, as Mr. Dalrymple was getting ready to leave, he said, "I came by tonight to see how you boys were getting along with my problem and to ask you to meet me at the house tomorrow afternoon at five o'clock. The lock on the secret room is set for that time."

"We'd be glad to," Frank replied. "After tonight we're especially eager to get inside the place ourselves."

As soon as the banker was gone, the boys helped Hurd Applegate into his car. Frank took the wheel and headed the old-fashioned automobile toward the big stone house on the bluff where Mr. Applegate lived. Joe followed in the Hardys' convertible.

As Frank started up the driveway, he noticed the front door was wide open and the lights on.

"Oh," Mr. Applegate said with alarm, "I remember now. I left it open when I ran out."

The boys parked the two cars, and shaken as he was, the old man hurried up the steps into the house ahead of them.

As he led the way into the library he stopped with a cry. "The chess set!" he gasped, clutching his heart. "I left it on the table! It's gone!"

CHAPTER VI

Waterfront Chase

JOE helped the shocked man sit down, then got him a drink of water. Frank, meanwhile, called the doctor.

While Joe stayed with Hurd Applegate, Frank entered the next room to check on the open safe he had spotted there. As he came back into the room, he heard Mr. Applegate, his eyes closed, whisper, "Rest of the jade in the safe."

Frank looked at Joe and shook his head. "Cleaned out," he said softly. "We'd better not tell him till after the doctor comes."

While they were waiting, the older boy called Chief Collig and reported what had happened.

"I think this second theft may be a cleverly planned part of the first one," Frank told him. "The thief got Hurd Applegate to open the safe and bring out his jade figurines. Then when he went back for the chess set the man fled, knowing Mr. Applegate would come after him. Once he was out of the house, it was easy for the thief's confederate to move in and take the chess set and rifle the open safe."

"Jade figurines!" the chief's voice crackled. "Reminds me of the harbor thieves. They've switched to small valuables. Anything they can slip into a pocket, or hide under a coat. They're still boarding the ships and getting into the warehouses. And this kind of loot is more precious than the bulky stuff."

"Yet they get off the piers with it," Frank put in.

"That's what beats us!" declared the chief angrily. "We frisk every person leaving the docks, and still the stuff gets out."

"But how can that be?" Frank asked, puzzled.

"I don't know. We spotted their black car, so they stopped using it," Chief Collig replied. "We're still watching all roads. Yet the stealing is worse than ever!"

"Hm," Frank considered. "This has been going on for months now, Chief. Has any of the loot turned up on the contraband market?"

"Nothing," the chief replied. "Still too hot to peddle. They're storing it some place."

While Frank had been talking to the police chief, the doctor had arrived and Joe had explained the situation quietly.

As Frank hung up, the medical man told the boys, "Mr. Applegate will be all right after a few days' rest. It's been a shock, though. I'll tell him about the rest of the missing jade tomorrow. No need for you to stay longer."

The boys thanked the doctor and promised the sick man they would help him get his property back. When they walked out to their car, the rain had stopped and the sky had cleared.

"You know," Frank said thoughtfully as he got behind the wheel, "Chief Collig says the harbor thieves are lifting small valuables now. There's a slim chance there might be a connection between the jade thieves and the harbor gang. What do you say we go down to the docks and have a look around?"

Joe agreed readily, and Frank headed the car along Shore Road toward town.

"Seems queer, so many things going on around the Purdy mansion all at once," Joe said. "First, Mr. Dalrymple's mystery, and next Hurd Applegate traced the jade thief there. Maybe those two cases are connected."

"Maybe all *three* mysteries are hooked up," said Frank thoughtfully.

In a short time the boys arrived at the waterfront. At least half a dozen freighters were tied up at the long piers that extended like fingers into the waters of Barmet Bay. In front of one vessel huge piles of freight were stacked on the dock in the glare of floodlights. The ship's cranes were busily swinging more cargo onto the pier.

"Must be a rush job," Frank commented as he parked the car.

The boys walked over to watch. There was a cool breeze from the sea and the tangy smell of salt water in the air.

Joe sniffed appreciatively. "Boy! Where are those harbor thieves? I'm ready for 'em!"

"Yes, but are they ready for you?" Frank said with a chuckle.

"You know the one I'd like to get my hands on," his brother added in high spirits. "The guy that almost ran us down yesterday!"

"Yes? What would you do to him?"

Joe considered his choice of punishment carefully. "Get him behind bars," he declared.

As the boys started to walk out on one of the docks, they were stopped by a weary-looking, steamship company guard in a gray uniform.

"Okay, you fellows. Where d'you think you're going?"

"We're just looking," Joe replied in a friendly tone.

"Well, you can't look here," the watchman said in a loud voice, which attracted a blue-shirted policeman nearby.

"Catch some of 'em, Charlie?" he asked, coming over. It was Officer Callahan. "Oh, it's the Hardy boys again. Let 'em in, let 'em in, Charlie!"

The boys thanked the policeman and started toward the black-hulled freighter. Frank and Joe watched the burly longshoremen moving some of its cargo away on hand trucks to the warehouses.

"The man who drove that limousine was husky," Joe recalled. "He easily could have been a longshoreman."

But Frank noticed that even these men were searched by Officer Callahan as they came off the pier. The boys boarded the freighter, and learned from the officers posted there that nothing had been missing that day.

Unhurriedly the Hardys moved from ship to ship. Police and company guards were on the alert everywhere. Frank and Joe walked back to the freighter from which merchandise was still being unloaded.

Several men on the deck were busy operating the huge cargo derrick. Suddenly, as the crane swung dockward with its load, a short, square-built man with a white sailor cap perched on his black, curly hair, leaped ten feet from the deck to the pier and dashed toward the warehouses.

"Hey!" cried the other men. "Stop!"

Instantly the whole area rang with the shrilling of police whistles. Frank noticed a suspicious bulge at the back of the man's baggy trousers.

Luckily, he and Joe were near enough to give chase. At the same time, Callahan and the watchman named Charlie came dashing onto the pier.

All four piled into the fugitive at once! Everybody went down. Arms and legs thrashed. Callahan got up first, dragging the laborer, wild-eyed and breathless, to his feet.

"Now," growled the officer. "Talk, you! Where is it?"

"Talk?" stammered the man in confusion.

"What's that in your back pocket?" Frank demanded.

"Why were you running away?" Joe asked tersely.

With a look of intense discomfort and dismay on his face, the man reached gingerly behind him. As Frank, Joe, and the two policemen watched eagerly, he brought out a brown paper bag, sodden and squishy.

"I'd promised to call my wife long-distance at seven o'clock and had forgotten. I was having a late supper, so I just put the rest of the food in my back pocket," he explained dolefully. "Three big, ripe pears. Sat down on it. Please, fellas, let me off. I've got to change my pants!"

In complete disgust Officer Callahan waved the man away. Frank and Joe, grinning at the ridiculousness of the scene, left the big commercial docks.

"Let's take a spin in the *Sleuth*," Frank proposed, referring to the brothers' motorboat. "Maybe we can pick up a clue by cruising around the harbor."

The boys pushed open the boathouse door, switched on the light, and looked with pride at their sleek craft. The *Sleuth* rocked gently on the water. The far door, opening on the bay, was down.

"Warm in here," Joe complained. "Funny, the sun's been gone for hours." He jumped into the boat and called, "Get the key, will you, Frank?"

Joe, proud of the craft, put his hand affectionately on the big motor. Quick as a flash he withdrew it.

"Hot!" he exclaimed, amazed. "Frank, somebody was using the *Sleuth* not long ago!"

CHAPTER VII

Crafty Thieves

QUICKLY Joe unscrewed the gasoline cap and peered into the tank of the Hardys' speedboat.

"Almost empty," he reported.

"That's not so strange," Frank reminded him. "Chet or Biff or one of the other fellows might have taken the *Sleuth* for a spin. Funny they didn't replace the gas, though."

As he spoke, Frank walked to the back of the boathouse and felt around on a small shelf, placed high up. Here the Hardy brothers had hidden a key for friends who might want to use their boat.

"Gone!" he exclaimed.

Meanwhile, Joe saw that the boat was, as usual, secured with its chain and padlock.

"Lucky I have the spare key in my pocket," said Frank. "We'd better gas up, then report this to the police."

"You think the *Sleuth* may have been 'borrowed' by the dock thieves?" Joe queried excitedly.

"Good chance, unless some pal of ours took a real long ride." Already Frank, kneeling, had unlocked the padlock and removed the chain.

"But why would the thieves keep the key?"

"Because our boat would always be available to them. Very handy, if you're a thief and need transportation in a hurry!"

Joe walked quickly to the front of the little building, and by pulling a rope, raised the door fronting on the bay.

"Suppose we look for some signs of the 'borrower' before we rush off," Frank advised.

He stepped into the front seat of the craft, and examined the compartments in the dashboard. Joe, meanwhile, checked every inch of the interior of the boathouse. But he found nothing. Turning, he saw his brother on his hands and knees under the rear seat of the *Sleuth*.

"What're you up to?"

"Here, steady the boat," was the reply. "Everything's sloshing around."

Like all such boats, the *Sleuth* had a wooden rack placed a few inches above the real bottom of the vessel, so that a certain amount of wash could be collected without the passengers' getting their feet wet. Frank was probing the murky water under the bars of the rack.

Suddenly he snatched up something. "Got it!"

With a triumphant smile, he handed his brother an empty matchbook.

" 'Bayport and Eastern Steamship Company,' " read Joe from the cover. "It's a clue, all right!"

The younger boy joined Frank and took the wheel of the craft. He switched on its powerful lights, and with a low purr the *Sleuth* headed out into the calm waters of Barmet Bay. The Hardys steered first for the dock of the Bayport Yacht Club, where they had the night pump attendant fill the fuel tank.

"Wait here!" said Frank, and he jumped to the dock, then dashed away and entered the clubhouse.

About fifteen minutes later Frank was back. Joe had spent the time checking the motor, which seemed to be in perfect condition.

"I called every single person who knew where that key was," Frank reported. "Nobody has used the boat in the past week, let alone tonight! It's a case of thievery, all right!"

Joe nodded, and started the motor. "Where to now?"

"Commercial docks."

Joe opened the throttle with a roar. The trim craft lifted her head and sprang forward. Twin arcs of white spray fell away from her bows. Heavy suds churned at her stern.

The whole bay was bathed in bright moonlight. Far ahead they could make out the black line of rock marking the edge of the harbor, and the open gap revealing its entrance from the ocean.

A short distance from shore lay the imposing white hulk of the *Sea Bright,* a passenger vessel which had just come from the Far East. Here and there floated buoys marking the channel for the ocean-going freighters. As the boys advanced, the whole harbor spread out astern of them. They could see the big ships in their piers, and over on the right, the wide mouth of Willow River, with the bridge crossing it.

"Where did the guy who borrowed our *Sleuth* take it?" Frank called to his brother above the sound of the motor. His eyes swept the horizon. "That's a big harbor!"

"You're not kidding!" Joe shouted. "Where else could they go?"

Frank pointed toward the mouth of Willow River. "Up there. It's navigable for miles and miles. And don't forget all the tributary streams."

"Whew! You think they went up there tonight in the *Sleuth?*"

"Could be!"

Joe piloted the craft out to the middle of the bay, then headed in toward the black hull of the freighter which was being unloaded. He nosed the boat smoothly in between two jetties. On one side was the pier where they had caught the laborer with the squashed lunch.

"We're in luck," Frank cried suddenly. "There's Chief Collig with Tomlin and Callahan!"

Bayport's chief of police had come to take charge of the case which had been vexing his department for months. He was pacing along the dock when he heard Frank shout:

"We picked up a lead, Chief!"

Carefully Joe brought the speedboat over to one of the huge piles, where Frank made her fast. In another moment the Hardys and the three policemen were standing in eager consultation.

"Somebody's been using our boat," Joe explained quickly as he handed over the matchbook. "We've a hunch it could be your thieves. One of them left this behind."

Chief Collig, a big, bluff man, tipped back his cap and examined the matchbook thoughtfully. Suddenly he made a wry face. With a broad palm he smacked his forehead.

"Great Scott!" he declared. "You're right, of course! Know why we haven't found these crooks on any boats, Officer Callahan?"

"No, sir," answered the policeman.

"Because they've taken to the water in well-known Bayport boats. We've been looking for strange craft! Frank and Joe, you've given us a real break. I'll get police launches out on the bay immediately!" He went off to phone orders and soon returned.

"See any unfamiliar people in pleasure boats around here?" Frank asked Officer Tomlin.

"Well," responded the policeman thoughtfully, "one or two launches I know were around earlier. There were men in them, but I didn't pay any particular attention—thought they were guests of the owners."

"Would you consider *our* boat suspicious?" Frank continued.

"Of course not."

"But that's the crooks' idea!" Chief Collig said. "I gave orders to check all boats and the people in 'em. I don't care if they've been cruising the bay for twenty years!"

At that moment a steamship company guard came over to the group. Seeing Frank and Joe, he gave a friendly nod. "Came back, eh?"

"We're back," Joe admitted with a sheepish smile. "Catch anybody else escaping with a ruined lunch?" He had mistaken the guard for Charlie, the one they had met earlier. But when the man looked mystified, Joe realized his mistake.

"Don't know about anybody's lunch," the guard said. "Weren't you two around here before, while it was raining, in that blue-and-white speedboat?" He peered at the brothers closely. Then he shrugged. "No, I guess it was a couple of older fellows. They waved to me when they were pushing off."

"Did you hear that, Chief Collig?" Frank exclaimed. "Whoever took our boat was snooping around here with it tonight, looking for a chance to steal something from one of the ships or warehouses."

Chief Collig immediately quizzed the guard. The man replied that the *Sleuth* had lingered in the harbor for some time. The two men had come on the docks briefly. "I didn't see 'em leave with anything," he concluded.

"Better check the warehouses and ships," advised Joe.

"Good idea," agreed the chief.

With that, he strode off the pier, and the other officers resumed their posts.

Frank turned to his brother. "I'll walk back to the car and drive home," he volunteered, "and bring back a new padlock for the *Sleuth*. That'll keep the thieves from using *our* boat, anyhow. This time we won't leave the key on the shelf."

"Right. I'll poke around here and see what I can dig up," Joe proposed.

Frank Hardy knew that his father, as a detective, had found it necessary to keep a supply of all sizes of locks—types that could not be opened by ordinary skeleton keys.

When he reached home Frank saw that all the windows were dark, except for a dim light in

Aunt Gertrude's bedroom. He let himself into the house quietly and tiptoed down to his father's basement workshop and chose a suitable lock. Suddenly the boy was startled by a voice demanding sharply:

"And just what do you think you're up to, young man?"

"Why—I was getting a lock, Aunt Gertrude."

"Lock! At this unearthly hour? What for?"

"To change the lock on the *Sleuth.*"

"Is that where you two were? On a boat ride? Frank Hardy, it is one-thirty in the morning!"

"I know, Auntie," he said cheerfully as he started for the stairs. "We'll tell you about it later. Don't worry."

"Don't worry!" she echoed tartly. "I'll only die of it!"

Frank grinned. "In a nutshell—thieves borrowed the *Sleuth* and took the key. We're going to lock them out—with this!" He held up the gadget. "We'll be home soon."

When he arrived at the harbor, Frank parked the convertible and strode swiftly onto the pier where he had left his brother. Only a few workers were left on the dock, but he could see no sign of Joe.

Frank hurried to the end where the boat had been moored, and peered into the water. The *Sleuth* was missing, too!

CHAPTER VIII

A Perilous Plunge

"LOOKING for your buddy?"

Frank whirled to face the same steamship company guard who had spotted the *Sleuth* hovering near the docks earlier.

"Yes! He's my brother. Have you seen him? Joe was supposed to wait for me."

"I kind of wondered about that," said the guard. "First he went all the way out to the edge of the pier and sat down. Just looking. All at once—about ten minutes ago—he comes running back here like crazy. Jumped in the blue-and-white boat and took off like a shot, straight out into the bay."

"Was Joe alone?" Frank asked quickly.

"All by himself."

"He must have seen something suspicious," Frank decided.

At that very moment Joe Hardy was bending tensely over the steering wheel of the *Sleuth*, which was cutting along at top speed. Her prow stuck far out of the water. Great waves of spray were thrown up on both sides.

But Joe seemed unconscious of the tremendous speed of his craft. His eyes were fixed with determination upon a powerful motorboat running several hundred yards straight in front of him. Two men were seated aboard, one at the wheel, the other looking back frequently as if nervous.

Ten minutes before, as Joe had sat at the edge of the dock, legs dangling, he had noticed this same boat bobbing beside the big white hull of the *Sea Bright*. One man had already boarded the motor craft and a second was climbing toward it down the ladder of the passenger vessel.

Suddenly Joe had leaned forward with sharp interest. In the moonlight he had seen the name on the prow of the motorboat. It was the *Napoli*, which belonged to Tony Prito's father. Joe had seen that neither of the pair in the boat was Mr. Prito or his son.

Now Joe heard a loud, whining roar, as the boat ahead picked up speed. Apparently the men realized they were being followed. The *Napoli* was showing her power.

"Come on, girl," Joe urged his own trusty

craft affectionately. He jammed the throttle wide open. The race was on!

Skimming over the smooth surface, throwing showers of glistening white spray, neither craft could gain on the other. Dark shapes of buoys marking the harbor channel shot by them. The wet, black rocks at the harbor's entrance came nearer and nearer, with the water of the Atlantic Ocean, lined with white crests of waves, just outside.

Squinting through the windshield, Joe considered his strategy. The fleeing boat was a swift one. But it would doubtless turn soon, and then, he knew, the lighter, easier-to-handle *Sleuth* would have the edge. He would cut them off without trouble.

To his amazement, however, the men held straight toward the mouth of the harbor. "They know their boat is heavier," Joe reasoned. "They're going out to sea, hoping I'll have to slow down or swamp among the swells!"

Already the big rocks were closing in on both sides. Ahead, the ocean waves broke with a resounding smash along the barrier. The *Napoli* veered crazily in and out among the closely placed harbor buoys.

"He doesn't know the channel!" flashed across Joe's mind. "He'll tear out the bottom on those submerged rocks." Frantically the boy sounded three long warning blasts on his own horn.

Too late! The other boat, trying to cut round the rocky point into the Atlantic, abruptly stopped short in the water as though a brake had been applied. A harsh grinding noise reached Joe's ears. Immediately the *Napoli's* hull settled stern first into the deep water.

Approaching the spot, Joe slowed down the *Sleuth*. But the two men had already jumped overboard, and after swimming a few strokes, splashed to shore and scrambled to the top of the breakwater. There, for a moment, they were silhouetted against the sky: a short, burly fellow and a slender man almost a foot taller.

"That short one looks like the man who drove the limousine!" Joe exclaimed, as both men quickly scampered off the embankment and disappeared.

Carefully Joe marked the position of the sunken boat. Then he turned the *Sleuth* back toward the piers. As he pulled in, Frank hailed him in relief.

"Say! What made you take off, anyway?"

"Plenty!" Joe gasped. "Wait'll you hear!"

The tide was coming in, and he scrambled onto the dock unaided. Breathlessly Joe poured out the story of the chase.

"And the short, burly man," he added, "was the driver of the limousine that almost ran us down!"

"Are you sure?" Frank asked.

"He looked back and I saw his face in the moonlight," Joe said.

"We must find Chief Collig," Frank said. "Maybe his men can still catch them."

Joe shook his head doubtfully. "Too easy for those fellows to lose themselves among the rocks along shore. They're free for the moment. But I know the spot where Tony's boat is!"

Just then Chief Collig walked onto the pier. The boys hurried over to him and described Joe's adventure.

"We'll salvage the *Napoli* first thing by daylight," the chief said. "How about coming along? Meet me at the police wharf."

The boys agreed at once and volunteered to call Tony Prito and tell him what had happened. Then Joe returned the *Sleuth* to her berth while Frank drove the car there to meet him. Together, they put the new lock on their craft.

In a short time they were both in the convertible and heading homeward through the deserted streets. A few minutes later they crawled wearily into bed.

But in a few hours the boys were up. Frank called Tony, who gasped in dismay. "The *Napoli!* That's a crime! . . . Yes, I'll go with you to see it."

The Hardys picked him up and they rode to the police wharf.

Chief Collig was waiting for them. "Sorry about

your boat, Tony. Those thieves are getting nervier by the minute."

"What about the Purdy place?" Joe asked him eagerly. "Did your men find anything when they searched last night?"

"Nothing," Collig replied wryly. "No thieves, no cars, no loot."

Just then a police boat equipped with a winch and cable for minor salvage operations came alongside the pier. The three boys and Collig clambered in, and the vessel headed for the mouth of the harbor.

Frank said, once more picking up the thread of the case, "Do you suppose Tony's boat was stolen by the same men who were seen in our boat earlier last night?"

"It wouldn't surprise me," Chief Collig answered.

"Anyhow," Joe spoke up, "we're pretty sure the short fellow in Tony's boat was the man who drove the limousine, and one of the harbor thieves. Sure like to know where he and his pal are hiding out."

By now the police boat had reached the mouth of the harbor. The officer at the wheel eyed the nearby shore warily.

"You're lucky you didn't stave your own boat in," he told Joe. "The underwater rocks are really treacherous along here."

"Don't I know it!" Joe agreed.

The officer throttled down and slowly approached the place that Joe indicated to him. A red harbor buoy bobbed nearby.

"I'm not going inside that marker," announced the pilot flatly, slowing to a halt.

"Where is the *Napoli* from here, Joe?" Tony asked.

"Just the other side of the red buoy, I'm afraid."

Around the police craft the water was clear and bluish green. Its surface was broken and dancing slightly from the effect of the waves outside the harbor. By leaning forward, the boys and Chief Collig made out a long white shape on the bottom.

"My boat! Can we get her up, Sergeant?" Tony questioned anxiously.

The second policeman assigned to the cruiser had been estimating their chances. "If we get her to the surface we can tow her in. The question is, *can* we get her to the surface? Looks pretty deep here to me. How are we going to put a line on her?"

Regretfully, the chief agreed. "You're right. We'll have to go back for a skin diver."

Here Joe broke in with a suggestion. "If I go down and attach a line, can you raise her with the winch?"

"But we haven't any diving equipment," protested the sergeant. "Not even a face mask."

"Faces were made before face masks," Joe observed, grinning. Already he had kicked off his shoes. Now he was pulling his shirt over his head, revealing his tan, lithe body. "Got your line ready?"

"You Hardys sure won't give up." Chief Collig nodded. "Okay. Try it."

The sergeant readied the salvage equipment. He extended the boom of his winch, then handed Joe a steel cable with a heavy steel hook at the end.

The boy was now stripped to a pair of white shorts. "I'm ready."

"I figure it's about twelve feet down," the sergeant told him gravely. "There'll be some pressure."

"And look out for the tow," Tony cautioned.

Joe accepted the cable. "I've done a lot of skin diving, and had experience with both," he assured them. "Any special place I should attach this?"

"Loop it around something solid on the *Napoli*, then snap the hook around the cable like this," the sergeant replied, demonstrating.

"Right."

With the cable in one hand, Joe climbed to the rail of the launch. There he balanced for a moment as he took a series of tremendous deep breaths. Then he plunged into the water.

Those on board the launch watched anxiously,

while the pilot tried to hold the boat steady. Joe soon became an indistinct blur against the sunken white craft.

Once submerged, Joe drove himself forward with powerful kicks. He kept his hands free for the cable. He began to feel the increasing pressure, mostly on his temples and chest. Joe penetrated deeper. Finally he could touch the *Napoli*.

Now he felt around it for a place to attach the cable. He moved forward and explored the front seat. There was no likely place—the steering wheel might rip out. Joe felt a pounding in his ears and he began to yearn for a breath of air. Still he groped around, feeling for something solid under the dashboard of the craft.

At this point Joe was directly under the steering wheel, the cable beneath his body. As he rolled over on his back to investigate the under part of the dashboard, the cable wound around his body. Suddenly and painfully, the cable had tightened against his flesh. The hook, that dangled from a length of cable in Joe's hand, had caught around a slat of the floor boards.

Joe yanked at the hook, but was unable to loosen it. He thrashed to release himself from the cable. But he was bound fast under the steering wheel, twelve feet below the water's surface!

CHAPTER IX

The Secret Room

BACK on the launch, Chief Collig, Frank, Tony, and the sergeant waited tensely.

"Hold this boat still!" Collig barked at the pilot.

"Sorry, Chief. She's drifting."

"The cable's gone taut," noted Tony. "Do you think Joe has attached it?"

"If he has, he ought to be up any second," Frank answered hopefully.

But the glittering surface of the water gave no sign of the swimmer underneath. More seconds passed.

"Something's wrong!"

As the words burst from Frank he, too, slipped out of his shoes and quickly stripped. In spite of anxiety for his brother, he was too wise to dive fully clothed.

Frank knifed into the cold water. With a powerful breast stroke, he swam quickly down to the *Napoli*. Almost immediately Frank spotted his brother's legs kicking from under the dashboard, and the steel cable encircling Joe's waist, holding him fast.

Shooting downward to the floor of the boat, Frank groped till his hand found the hook caught in the floor boards. With a tug he released it, flung away the line, grabbed Joe, and propelled him to the surface.

As Joe's head and shoulders popped above water, he exhaled, then gasped in a lungful of air, too exhausted to swim. The strong arms of Chief Collig and Tony hauled Joe into the boat. He lay on the deck, breathing heavily.

Meanwhile, Frank's head bobbed into view. "Joe okay? Hold steady. I'll fix the cable."

"You come out of there," Chief Collig roared, "before *you* almost drown!"

But Frank was already well under water. Seizing the hook, he stroked toward the prow of the *Napoli*. There he detected a steel eye for mooring. Passing the hook through it, he looped the cable again, and surfaced.

"Grind away," he called cheerfully to the sergeant at the winch. Then he climbed aboard.

By this time Joe was sitting up and slapping the water out of his ears. Chief Collig shook his head. "It's lucky there are *two* of you left!"

"I second that," Joe said weakly. "Thanks for the rescue, brother."

Now the engine of the winch began grinding. The steel cable was reeled in steadily. The *Napoli* rose toward the surface like a big, inert fish. Quickly the pilot started the launch's engines and pulled away. The disabled craft trailed behind, half under water.

Back at the police wharf, Tony was informed that his boat could be repaired, although he would be without the use of it for a while.

"I wonder if the gang used the *Sleuth* to steal anything," Joe said, in a worried voice, as he, Tony, and Frank left the wharf with the chief.

"Prepare yourself for a shock," advised Chief Collig. "Last night there was a big theft from the captain's cabin on one of these passenger ships. We've been keeping it quiet, hoping for a lead."

"Whew!" Frank gave a whistle. "What ship?"

"The *Sea Bright,* under Captain Stroman's command." Here Chief Collig paused deliberately. "That ship is owned by the Bayport and Eastern Steamship Company."

Instantly Joe remembered the matchbook. "Then it *was* our *Sleuth* they used," he declared.

Frank observed a familiar look in their old friend's eyes. "Chief," the boy asked suddenly, "what did the gang steal?"

"They stole," Collig pronounced slowly, "a

very valuable jade necklace, which the captain had bought for his wife."

It took a split second for this information to hit home. Both Hardys exclaimed together:

"Hurd Applegate! His stolen collection!"

Chief Collig signified agreement. "First thing I thought of. Two thefts of jade within a few hours. It's only logical the same person is responsible."

"Where's Captain Stroman now?" Frank asked. "Can we talk to him? Does he know what the thief looked like?"

"Whoa! He's gone to New York to consult with the insurance company. He'll be back tomorrow."

"All this begins to fit together," Joe pointed out thoughtfully. "Mr. Applegate's case *is* tied up with the old Purdy mansion."

"Yes," Chief Collig agreed. "But how?"

"Getaway by water!" Frank answered excitedly. "The Willow River runs right behind the Purdy property. These crooks can go there from the docks without touching dry land."

"And that's where they transfer the loot to cars or trucks!" Joe finished eagerly.

"Look, Chief," Frank said, "Joe and I are going out to the mansion at five o'clock." The youth checked his watch. "It's almost noon now. We'll see if we can turn up anything there, and get in touch with you afterward."

On the way home the boys dropped Tony Prito off at his father's construction company. As he got out of the car he thanked the Hardys again for their help in raising the *Napoli,* and Frank and Joe wished him good luck with the repairs.

When they reached home, Aunt Gertrude was waiting in the living room. "I never know when you're coming back, or if you're coming back at all," she complained at once, heading for the kitchen. "So you needn't be surprised if there isn't much lunch ready!"

Frank winked at Joe. A moment later Miss Hardy entered the dining room with a tray of sandwiches, relishes, potato salad, chocolate milk, and a whole fudge cake.

"This is all there is," she announced, and sat down with her nephews.

The boys grinned. During the meal Frank and Joe told her in detail about their adventures the night before and that morning. She snorted and clucked and shook her head, but the boys knew she was enjoying every word of it.

The brothers spent the afternoon making and studying notes about the case. At four thirty they headed the yellow convertible toward the Purdy mansion.

When they reached the estate, Frank parked his car behind the high bushes on the other side of Willow River Road, where Hurd Applegate had hidden his old automobile.

"No use being conspicuous," Joe said approvingly.

The brothers got out and walked to the heavy wooden gate. Frank gave a low whistle of surprise. "We left this open last night. Now it's closed."

Cautiously the Hardys slipped through.

"I want to check for footprints behind the house again," Frank said as they kept to the trees along the drive. "That shut gate means somebody's been coming or going."

"Probably the police closed it after they searched last night," Joe said.

"That's true," Frank replied. "But I want to look, anyway."

He made his way to the path in the woods where he had first seen footprints. Frank stooped to examine the ground.

"New footprints," he announced. "Quite a few of them. Look at those deep ones. A heavy-set fellow must have made them. Could be the limousine driver—the one you saw in the *Napoli!*"

"You're sure those aren't the same tracks you found yesterday?" Joe inquired doubtfully.

"Couldn't be—not after all that rain. No, these are fresh."

The young sleuths followed the trail among the trees down to the water. At this point the river was fairly wide. The boys looked for signs of a boat. A minute later they heard the sound of an automobile engine coming from the driveway.

"It may be Mr. Dalrymple," Joe said tersely. "But it could be the harbor thieves. We'd better sneak up."

The boys left the path and picked their way noiselessly through the thick green brush until they had reached a spot at the side of the house. From there, they could see the front porch.

A tall man in a lightweight suit and straw hat, obviously impatient, stood in the yard before the house, glancing around. Several times he looked directly at the boys' hiding place but failed to see them.

"Dalrymple?" Joe breathed. "Or his double?"

Next time the man turned his back, they ran silently forward and stopped just behind him. Joe touched his shoulder.

"What!" the man spun around.

"Mr. Dalrymple," Joe greeted him. "Sorry! But we wanted to be sure who you were."

"You boys did give me a start," the banker confessed. "I didn't see your car, so thought you weren't here. But come along. We can't waste a minute. The time lock is set for five o'clock exactly. We have to get in now, or lose our chance."

The banker opened the front door with his key. After a hasty look into the living room, which contained the grandfather's clock the Hardys had seen through the window the night before, they hurried upstairs.

"Another warning!" he cried out, snatching up
the paper

"The secret room is down the hall," Mr. Dalrymple explained.

Briskly the banker entered a sitting room. While the boys watched, fascinated, he pushed aside a small framed photograph and put his fingernail into a tiny hole behind it. A very small round door opened, revealing the dials of a time lock!

After twirling these, Mr. Dalrymple stepped back. Before the boys' eyes, what had seemed a line in the wallpaper now developed into a crack that grew wider and wider as a door swung outward.

"The entrance to the secret room!" Frank thought.

Mr. Dalrymple stepped through into a small, windowless chamber. Frank, then Joe, followed closely. Joe was the first to spot a folded sheet of white paper in the exact center of the rug.

"Another warning!" he cried out, snatching up the paper.

In stunned silence, Frank, Joe, and Mr. Dalrymple read the penciled warning:

"Death while the clock ticks!
This is your last warning!"

CHAPTER X

The Shadowy Figures

FRANK examined the threatening message for fingerprint smudges, but there were none. The lettering was like that of the first two warnings.

"We'll keep this note if you don't mind, Mr. Dalrymple," he said. "May need it as evidence."

The banker nodded gravely. "You know, boys," he said, "it's not so much the threat of death that bothers me. It's the idea that somebody hates me enough to want to kill me! Who could it be?"

Frank and Joe, too, wondered about the motive behind the strange notes.

"What about robbery?" Joe ventured. "Has anything been disturbed?"

Quickly Mr. Dalrymple riffled through the papers on his table, and then checked his filing cabinet.

"No," he muttered. "Same as before—a mysterious note in the middle of the floor. But nothing has been touched."

Frank Hardy looked carefully around the square, windowless room. "Well," he said, "if someone is going in and out, we ought to be able to find out how! Please close the door, Mr. Dalrymple. Let's get busy, Joe."

The banker pressed a switch, turning on an overhead light. Then he pulled shut the heavy, steel-plate door.

The Hardys went into action. First, Frank walked to the fireplace and peered up the chimney.

"You're right, sir, it's barred," he observed. "The opening's too small for even a baby to come down. No intruder came in this way."

Joe took a small mallet from his pocket and tapped the walls gently for a hollow sound. Meantime, Frank rolled up the rug and checked the floor for a trap door or movable boards. The entire room, however, seemed perfectly tight.

"It doesn't make sense!" Frank declared. "Somebody got in here with those notes."

"I know." Mr. Dalrymple sighed.

"One more possibility," said Frank abruptly. He pulled a tape measure from his pocket and quickly took the dimensions of the room. Then he said, "Now, Mr. Dalrymple, will you let us out?"

The banker opened the secret door and Frank

took a measurement of the wall's thickness. After they left the secret room, Mr. Dalrymple closed the door, set the time lock, and replaced the photograph. Meanwhile, Frank was measuring the sitting room. Then he slipped into the hall and measured that.

"What's the idea?" the banker asked.

For a moment the boy calculated swiftly in his head. "I thought there might be some kind of secret passage behind the vault," he explained. "But it's impossible. All the measurements check out."

"I guess we're stumped," Joe admitted ruefully. "But you'd better take the warning seriously, Mr. Dalrymple. Stay away from here unless we're with you."

The three descended the long, wide stairway in silence. Pausing at the bottom, they were startled by the only sound audible in the big, empty house.

Tick-tock! Tick-tock! Tick-tock!

" 'Death while the clock ticks'!" Joe exclaimed, and bolted across the hall into the living room. There stood the tall grandfather's clock, its pendulum swinging steadily. *Tick-tock!*

Mr. Dalrymple wrinkled his forehead. "I never wind that clock," he declared.

"*Somebody* has," Joe said. "It was going last night when we were here. Maybe the same person who's writing the notes winds it. He says he's going to kill you while the clock ticks and he might mean this very one! We'll spoil his game whatever it is!"

Joe looked into the glass door of the lower case where the pendulum hung. Nothing lay inside. He cautiously opened the upper door and peered into the works behind the face.

"Nothing here," he announced.

Suddenly Frank remembered something. "Mr. Dalrymple," he said, "do you have a set of keys for us?"

The banker looked dismayed. "Oh, tosh!" he exclaimed. "I've so much on my mind. I forgot all about it. I'll have them made first thing tomorrow."

A short time later the boys' yellow convertible rolled up the Hardy driveway and into the garage. From directly overhead came the sound of loud laughter, people talking, and a series of heavy bumps on the floor.

"What's going on!" Joe exclaimed. The brothers rushed upstairs.

The door of the Hardys' laboratory opened on the spectacle of Jerry Gilroy rolling about on the floor. Chet Morton seemed about to step on Jerry with his whole weight. Tony Prito and Biff Hooper were howling with delight, and Phil Cohen was photographing the scene with one of Joe's cameras.

"Strong stomach muscles, you say?" Chet

roared. "Hold still, and I'll test 'em for you."

"No! No!" pleaded Jerry. "Not that. They're *weak*. I give in!"

Phil Cohen was the first to notice the newcomers.

"Gentlemen!" he cried out. "There will be a moment of silence while we all observe the arrival of the Hardy boys! Look at them closely, gentlemen! Feast your eyes! Do not neglect this opportunity. For the Hardys come, and the Hardys go, but what they're up to, does anybody know?"

"Hear, hear—poetry!" Tony applauded.

"Does anybody know what the Hardys *are* up to?" repeated Phil, gesturing like an orator. "I wait for a reply."

"*I* have one, and it's not about the harbor thieves." Jerry grinned. "I think Frank and Joe are going romantic. Did you see 'em ducking out with their girls in the moonlight last night?"

"Sure enough," Chet drawled. "I also heard from Iola that soon as they were on the porch, Frank and Joe made a break for the car. Iola says she and Callie don't know what it was all about, but it had better be mighty important!"

Joe looked noncommittal. "Well, you can tell her it was."

Their stout friend moved closer, with a glint in his eye. As the Hardys well knew, Chet's curiosity was almost as great as his appetite.

"Sure, pals," he went on. "If I can just get a few details, I'm sure the girls will—er—be very much interested. Let's see—you couldn't stay at the party because you had to go out to the old Purdy place . . ."

Frank and Joe smiled at Chet's effort to coax information from them. Though he was sometimes afraid, he liked nothing better than to be included in their adventures.

"Is that right?" Frank inquired casually. "Tell us more, Chet."

"You went to the Purdy place because . . . because . . . uh . . . old Purdy buried all his money out there and you're looking for it!" Chet had to grin at his own bluff.

"Nice try!" Joe laughed.

"Oh, leave 'em alone," Jerry Gilroy said good-naturedly. "We'll wake up some morning and read all about it in the papers."

But Chet Morton persisted. "Aw, come on, fellows. Aren't you going to let me in on your case?"

"Guess you'll have to turn detective yourself," Joe teased, shaking his head.

"You look out," Chet warned them. "I might just do that! Meanwhile, it's suppertime. Let's go, everybody."

When he and the other boys had departed in Jerry's jalopy, Frank and Joe stayed in the lab and discussed the mystery until Aunt Gertrude summoned them to eat. Afterward, the brothers decided to visit the Purdy house.

"Even if we don't have a key, we'll see if there's any activity out there tonight," Joe said.

Frank agreed. "Let's walk. We can take a short cut."

The brothers waited until it was dark. After equipping themselves with flashlights, they started out at a rapid pace in the bright moonlight. Soon they had left the town behind. Once on Willow River Road, they hugged one side, and when cars passed, the boys melted into the brush to avoid detection.

As they reached the Purdy gate, Joe crouched and looked back. The road lay clear and pale in the moonlight, but the long ivy-covered wall was shadowy and dark.

"Hey, Frank!" he whispered. "Somebody just ducked from one tree to another back there. We're being trailed!"

"Let him follow," Frank answered. "We'll hide in the bushes near the house and spy on *him*."

Quickly the brothers scrambled over the gate. Soon they were well concealed in the same spot from which they had first seen Mr. Dalrymple that afternoon. They could see both the front and back doors of the high old house, with its slate roofs gleaming in the moonlight.

Minutes passed in silence. Then a heavy-set figure sneaked across the open space in front of the house. Frank and Joe watched tensely. The figure slipped stealthily around to the back. Here the windows were closer to the ground. As the intruder raised his head to peer in, moonlight fell full upon his face.

"Chet Morton!" Joe hissed, astonished. "We'd better get hold of him before—"

"Sh!" Frank signaled tersely. "Somebody else coming!"

A white-shirted figure now came from the woods and approached the back of the house. The man walked swiftly, as though sure of his way. At the same time, Chet backed cautiously away from the window—until he had backed right into the stranger!

"Eeek! Help!" Chet cried shrilly.

At this outcry the white-shirted figure turned and dashed for the woods.

"After him!" Frank shouted, breaking cover. "He's heading for the river!"

Frank and Joe plunged down the path they had discovered earlier. But already an outboard motor was kicking into life. The brothers raced to the river's edge in time to see a small green boat carrying one man put-put out onto the bright, moonlit water.

The man crouched in the stern, anxiously watching the shore. The moonlight revealed his features.

"The limousine driver!" Joe exclaimed.

CHAPTER XI

A Suspicious Captain

BOTH boys stared after the motorboat, now only a dark spot in the distance. It was headed down the river toward the bay. Soon it had disappeared around a bend.

"Are you sure it was the limousine driver?" Frank demanded.

"Positive. It's the third time I've seen him. This proves our theory, Frank. The harbor thieves are using this house. Are they responsible for the scream and the warning notes?"

Just then they heard a rustle of brush from the top of the wooded path. "Frank . . . Joe?" called Chet's quavering voice. "Is that you I hear talking?"

"No!" Frank shouted laughingly. "We're two ghosts!"

Switching on their flashlights, the brothers

climbed back up the path. "Hi, detective!" Joe greeted a somewhat crestfallen Chet Morton revealed in the beam of his flashlight. "What's the big idea of scaring off our quarry?"

"*Oh-h,*" Chet moaned. "Me—scaring *him!* I was standing here, and this ghostly white thing—"

"What you're talking about is a man in a white T-shirt," Frank wryly informed him. "And, thanks to you, he's made a clean getaway down the river."

Joe made a grimace of mock despair. "What were you up to, tailing us?"

In a meek voice Chet explained. "When you said I'd have to turn detective to find out about your case, I took your advice. So I shadowed you out here all the way from your house."

"Okay, you win, Chet," Frank sighed.

The three boys started together down Willow River Road for home. "You might as well work with us. Better give us a day or two, though. By then we should have an assignment for you— Detective Morton."

The chunky boy agreed with alacrity. A block from their house Chet picked up his jalopy.

"We'll keep you posted," Frank promised him.

The next morning, immediately after breakfast, the boys drove downtown to the Bayport and Eastern Steamship Company offices.

"Captain Stroman?" repeated the secretary at the reception desk. "Yes, he's here, boys, but I'm afraid he's too occupied to see you."

"Tell the captain it's about a jade necklace," Frank said.

The girl gave the Hardys a startled look and retreated to an inner office. She returned shortly and directed them to go in.

A tall, red-haired man, wearing the black uniform of the merchant marine, with gold bars and stars on the sleeve to indicate his master's rank, stood behind a heavy mahogany desk. Before the Hardys had a chance to speak, Captain Stroman demanded gruffly:

"What do you boys know about the jade necklace?"

"Nothing yet, sir," Frank answered. "We were hoping you would tell us about the theft."

"Why should I? Who are you, anyhow?"

Quickly Frank introduced himself and Joe, then went on, "We have a motorboat here at the harbor, a blue-and-white outboard called the *Sleuth*."

"What?" the captain's eyes narrowed suspiciously. "A blue-and-white boat? Just a minute!" Watching the boys closely, he picked up a telephone. "Give me police headquarters. Chief Collig."

"Wait! You don't understand!" Joe protested.

Frank restrained his brother. "Maybe it'll be easier this way."

"Chief Collig?" the captain spoke into the

phone. "Two boys named Hardy are in my office. Say they own that boat my mate spotted hanging around the *Sea Bright* the night of the theft. They're asking about the jade. I'll hold them till you get here. . . . What? What's that you say?"

By the captain's change of expression from suspicion to amazement, Frank and Joe could tell that Chief Collig was setting him straight on the events of the day in question.

"Right, Chief," said Stroman and hung up. He turned to the boys and said, "Seems I've made a mistake. When you lose a rare collector's item that has taken you a lifetime to find, you're apt to be suspicious of people. I apologize."

"Chief Collig told us you'd gone to the insurance company," Frank said.

The captain nodded. "They're putting a private detective on the case immediately." He paused. "By the way, what *is* your interest in this matter?"

"A friend of ours had a jade collection stolen the night before last," Joe explained. "We think your necklace may have been taken by the same man. Did you happen to get a look at him?"

"Unfortunately, no. It was the busy time of night and I was superintending the unloading of cargo. Several new dock workers were on board. Any one of them might have slipped unnoticed into my cabin."

"But what's this about the *Sleuth?*" Frank queried.

"My mate saw your boat, but thought nothing of it at the time. There were two men aboard. The mate had only a brief glimpse of them."

Though disappointed at the captain's lack of further information, Frank and Joe promised to do all they could to recover the precious jade. When they were outside, Frank suggested that they make the rounds of the art and jewelry stores in Bayport to see if the thieves had tried to sell any of the jade. They started near the docks where there were a number of shops specializing in imported and unusual goods. The two made queries in one after another. None of the dealers, however, had bought any jade objects within the past two months.

"We'll move uptown," Joe said.

Doggedly they went to two large stores of the same type in the center of Bayport. Still no results.

"If I'd stolen a valuable collection," Joe said suddenly, "I wouldn't try to sell it here, either."

"Well—where would you go?"

"To Mr. Swarts!" Joe declared.

"Of course!" Frank exclaimed. "Just the place! Let's go!"

Quickly he headed their car across town to a little out-of-the-way antique shop which the boys had checked for stolen goods on several occasions. Frank parked in front of the drab brick building, and the boys hurried down the steps to a small store below street level. In the window piles of odds and ends were jumbled with genuine treasures.

As they entered, a gray-haired man with steel-rimmed spectacles looked at them across a wooden counter.

"Hello, boys!" he called in greeting.

"Good morning, Mr. Swarts," said Joe. "Say, has anybody tried to sell you some fine jade lately?"

The man started. "Funny you should ask that. Fellow was in just this morning, early. He had a nice set of chessmen and a necklace with him."

"Did you buy them?" Joe asked eagerly.

"Ho, ho! No." Mr. Swarts laughed. "He wanted too much for them. Needed money, he said. So? Am I supposed to overpay him out of charity?"

"What did he look like, Mr. Swarts?"

The owner considered a moment. "Oh, big tall fellow, middle-aged, wore rimless glasses. Had on a summer suit and straw hat."

"Sounds like Mr. Dalrymple!" Frank exclaimed.

"Oh—you know him?" asked the proprietor, mistaking the reason for their outburst. "Good. I just remembered these."

He fished in his pocket, then laid on the counter a little chain with three keys. "See that he gets these back, will you?"

Joe glanced at the keys quickly and pocketed them. "I certainly will!"

After thanking the man, the Hardys hastened from the store to the convertible.

"How do you like that!" Joe exclaimed. "Must have been Mr. Dalrymple's double. *He* had the chessmen *and* the necklace! That proves one gang pulled both thefts!"

"Let's see those keys," Frank said, starting the car. "Hey! I recognize one."

"You bet!" his brother crowed. "It's the key to the old lock on the *Sleuth!* We'll soon find out about the other two. Make tracks fast to our laboratory, driver!"

"Yes, *sir!*" responded Frank in high spirits.

Soon the car pulled into the Hardy driveway. Before they could start upstairs to the lab, however, the kitchen door slammed. The thin, energetic figure of Aunt Gertrude fairly flew at them.

"*There* you are! What are you up to? Oh, I knew when your parents went to Maine, there'd be trouble. Don't stand there gaping. Out with it!"

"Aunt Gertrude," Frank begged, "out with what?"

"No use trying to hide it. A private detective has just been here—to investigate you boys!"

CHAPTER XII

Meteor Special

SPEECHLESS, Frank and Joe could only stare at each other. Nervously Aunt Gertrude continued:

"Imagine! A strange man coming to this house and asking all kinds of questions as though you were criminals!"

The boys piloted their excited aunt into the kitchen and made her sit down.

"What kind of 'investigation' do you think this is?" Joe asked his brother with keen curiosity.

"Maybe the fellow was from the insurance company," Frank suggested. "Captain Stroman probably reported the *Sleuth* incident to him. Can you tell us more about it now, Auntie?"

Miss Hardy composed herself. "I was dusting the living room when the doorbell rang. A young man stood there and said his name was Mr. Smith."

"Mr. Smith!" Joe hooted. "How phony can you get?"

Aunt Gertrude continued, "He said, 'I'm a private eye.' Then he flashed a wallet at me and showed his credentials."

"Private eye!" Joe repeated indignantly. "He's been reading too many corny detective stories."

"What does this Mr. Smith look like, Aunt Gertrude?" Frank asked.

"Well he's about thirty, I'd say. Not tall, not short. He wore a nice suit, and a gray fedora hat. And . . . he had a little toothbrush mustache!"

"Was it false?" Joe queried.

"How should I know?" their aunt snapped, her energetic self again. "I didn't study him through a magnifying glass!"

"That's what we need now," said Frank. "A magnifying glass." He looked at Joe significantly. "Because I think we have the *keys* to this mystery!"

In answer, Joe jingled his pocket. "Let's go!"

"Don't you dare!" cried Aunt Gertrude. "No detective work until you have a decent lunch."

The brothers were famished, and gladly complied. Twenty minutes later there was not a crumb left of the roast-beef sandwiches and the apple pie Miss Hardy had made.

"Delicious, Auntie," Frank declared.

"Thanks for stopping us," Joe added.

Their aunt beamed. The boys excused themselves and hastened to their lab. Joe brought out the three keys for examination.

"The first is the key to the *Sleuth* all right," Frank confirmed, fitting it to the original lock. "This second one is the kind used in ordinary door locks."

"The third is an automobile ignition key," Joe reported. "We'll soon find out what kind of car it's for."

In Fenton Hardy's laboratory next to the boys', he kept a photograph file of ignition keys for all automobiles of domestic and foreign manufacture. Frank and Joe went to compare these to the key dropped by Mr. Dalrymple's mysterious double at Swarts' shop.

"Start with the American makes," Frank proposed, "and take this year's models first."

The suggestion proved a good one. In less than five minutes the key had been identified as belonging to the current year's Meteor Special.

"The Special—that's the *big* Meteor—the limousine!" Joe noted with excitement. "Frank, it could have been the car that nearly hit us!"

"And there probably aren't too many of them around," Frank reasoned. "The next step is to find out who owns Meteor Specials in this area. We'll need police help."

Joe agreed. He suggested that Frank make the trip to headquarters. "I want to stay here and do some lab work. Mr. Dalrymple lent me those first two threatening notes. Let me have the third one. I'll do a handwriting analysis on it."

Accordingly, Frank drove to the handsome stone building that housed Bayport's police headquarters. He was allowed to see Chief Collig immediately.

"Anything new on the harbor thieves?" Frank asked.

"Yes," the chief replied tersely. "As you recall, Joe reported he'd seen a man climbing down from the *Sea Bright* into the *Napoli* just before he went after it. I had Captain Stroman check his ship to be sure that nothing more was gone. None of the crew reported anything missing, so we assumed the thieves came away empty-handed that time."

"Didn't they?" Frank asked.

"They did not. They took a diamond ring and several fine gold gifts from one of the crew members."

"Why wasn't it noticed before?" Frank queried.

"The night the jade was stolen, the sailor was taken ill suddenly and removed to sick bay. He had left his locker standing open when he was stricken. Of course he didn't miss his valuables until he returned to his quarters this morning."

Frank looked serious. "The thieves must have spotted that open locker when they took the jade, but were afraid to take the time to go through it."

The chief nodded. "So they came back. They're

getting bolder and bolder!" Collig frowned deeply. "Well," he said, "you wouldn't be down here, Frank, unless you'd turned up something."

Frank told him what they had found out at Swarts' antique store, and of the keys dropped by the man resembling Mr. Dalrymple.

"Good work!" exclaimed Chief Collig. "So the fellow was trying to peddle Stroman's necklace and Applegate's chess set! That certainly links the two thefts."

Frank nodded. "Look at this key. It's the ignition key to a late model Meteor Special."

Chief Collig understood immediately. "Very likely the car the harbor thieves used!"

"Right," Frank agreed. "Could we get a list of all the owners of such cars in the area? Then we can check them out, one by one."

"I'll call the State Motor Vehicle Bureau right away." The chief looked troubled. "With all my men in the harbor, I can't spare anybody to run down this lead."

"We'll take care of that," Frank promised, "as soon as you can give me the owners' names."

Relieved, Chief Collig remarked with a smile, "So Captain Stroman suspected at first you were crooks?"

"That's not all." Frank laughed and briefly told of "Mr. Smith's" call on Aunt Gertrude.

Here the chief eyed Frank with a twinkle. "And how's your other business coming?"

"What other business, Chief?"

"The appointment you had yesterday at the Purdy place—"

He was interrupted by the buzzing of the desk telephone. The policeman picked up the instrument and listened a moment.

"For you," he said, handing over the phone.

"Frank?" Joe's tone was insistent.

"What's up?"

"Can't tell now. Just get home—fast."

Frank drove back as rapidly as he could through the afternoon traffic. He found Joe and Aunt Gertrude in the living room.

"One thing after another," Miss Hardy was complaining. "First that private eye, and now this! It's *enough* to make a person wish she didn't have a detective in the family."

"What happened?" Frank demanded. Joe's face was serious as he handed his brother a sheet of stationery.

"Came in the mail just now," Joe said, "addressed to Aunt Gertrude."

Frank read the warning scrawled on the sheet.

"If you value your nephews' lives, tell them to mind their own business."

"A death threat," Aunt Gertrude declared vehemently. "Now maybe you'll give up chasing harbor thieves!"

"Not a chance, Auntie!" Joe exclaimed. "I checked the handwriting. This note was written by the same person who threatened Mr. Dalrymple!"

"Oh, my lands, what's the difference? It's still a death threat!" Aunt Gertrude cried.

"There's a big difference," Joe stated. "I'm *glad* you got this letter."

His aunt stared at him in bewilderment but Frank nodded understanding. "I get it," he said. "We thought we weren't making headway on Mr. Dalrymple's case. This note proves that we are. We have somebody worried!"

"You have *me* worried." Aunt Gertrude sighed. "Mr. Dalrymple is in danger and so are you!"

At that moment the telephone rang. Aunt Gertrude started. "If it's another threat—" She broke off as Frank took the call. He picked up a pencil from the stand and jotted something on a pad.

"That was Chief Collig," Frank announced after he had hung up. "The motor vehicle office has eight owners of Meteor Specials registered in this area. Here's the list. One is a Mr. Henry Nichols, who lives closest to us. Come on, Joe. Let's go!"

CHAPTER XIII

The Eavesdropper

MR. HENRY NICHOLS' home turned out to be a large one in Bayport's most attractive residential section.

"Frank!" Joe grabbed his brother's arm and pointed to the garage. Showing through the open door were the black fenders and shining grille of a new Meteor Special!

"Good afternoon, boys!" called an old man seated in a rocking chair on the front porch. "Hot weather."

"Sure is," Frank agreed. "Are you Mr. Nichols?"

"Yes sirree." The old man was very thin and weak looking, but his light-blue eyes were lively.

"I've been Henry Nichols seventy-nine years, now; eighty next April. Never minded it either, 'cept when I was young. Then I used to wish I was somebody famous—"

"Henry!" called a voice just inside the screen door. "That's enough!" A small, white-haired woman stood there. "What is it you boys want?"

Frank said politely, "We came to ask about your car."

"Don't drive those machines myself," Mr. Nichols piped up. "*I* drove a team of horses and did some harness racing."

Mrs. Nichols interrupted proudly, "Boys, *I* drive the car."

"How do you like your Meteor Special?" Joe asked her.

"Rides nice. And it's fast. I love a speedy car!"

Frank and Joe were amused by the couple, but did not smile. "Do a lot of driving?" Frank asked.

"Well, shopping downtown, and to church."

Mr. Nichols chuckled. "When Ma gets to going, I say to myself, 'Henry, buckle your seat belt!' "

Frank and Joe grinned, but thought Mrs. Nichols' Meteor clearly was not the one they were after. "Thanks for your time," Frank said to the couple. "We're very much interested in Meteor Specials."

Back in their convertible, the Hardys looked at the seven remaining names on the list. It was now late in the afternoon.

"We'd better split up, if we're going to cover these people," Frank advised. "I'll drive you home, so you can get Dad's car."

When the Hardys returned home from their quest, each reported no luck. None of the owners of Meteor Specials had resembled Mr. Dalrymple.

"There's one possible answer," Frank deduced. "The car this key belongs to may have been brought here from a distance. Probably it's using stolen plates."

"Yes, but where *is* it?" Joe wondered.

The young detectives were forced to go to bed with the question unanswered.

The next morning after breakfast Frank and Joe found a bright and eager Chet Morton seated on the Hardy doorstep. "You said to give you a day or two, so here I am!" he announced.

"Right on schedule." Joe grinned as the brothers sat down with their friend. They told him of their efforts to catch the harbor thieves, solve Mr. Dalrymple's mystery, and find the missing jade articles.

"Wow! I can hardly keep 'em all straight!" said the stout boy. "Well, I'll be on the lookout for that Meteor Special!"

"Good," responded Joe. "If you spot it, let us know on the double."

"Count on me!" Raising his right hand, and placing his left over his heart, Chet declaimed, "Let it never be said that Chet Morton forsook his companions in the hour of distress. Let the thieves do their worst! Chet Morton defies them!"

"Okay, okay!" Frank laughed. "Is Chet Morton ready to go now?"

"Lead on," Chet said, waving. "I follow. But where?"

"To see Mr. Dalrymple," Frank replied. "It's time he knew his property's being used by the harbor thieves."

"And we'll show him the warning that was sent to Aunt Gertrude," Joe added.

Soon the Hardys' convertible was carrying the three boys along the highway from Bayport to Lakeside. Once in town, they drove to the leading bank, of which Mr. Dalrymple was an officer.

He received the boys in his office, and listened intently as the Hardys told of their suspicions.

"Criminals using *my* house!" he exploded. "Outrageous! But it explains the notes. Those thieves are trying to scare me away, and you boys, too!"

"Yes," Frank agreed. "But it still doesn't explain *how* the messages were put into the time-locked room."

"That's true," the banker admitted. "What else have you found?"

Frank described the theft of the jade necklace Captain Stroman had purchased for his wife in the Orient. "Probably by the same thief who stole Hurd Applegate's collection."

To the boys' surprise, Mr. Dalrymple disagreed sharply. "No connection at all!" he snapped.

"I'm convinced that Applegate is suffering from hallucinations. His whole story is preposterous!"

The boys rose to leave, promising to keep the banker posted. To their disappointment, he had again forgotten to have a set of house keys made. Back on the road to Bayport, the young detectives considered Dalrymple's remark about Mr. Applegate.

"What do you think, Frank?" Joe asked. "Did Hurd Applegate *really* lose any jade?"

Frank said emphatically, "I think Mr. Dalrymple's still angry about being called a thief. But it won't hurt to have another talk with Mr. Applegate."

Suddenly both Hardys noticed that Chet's attention had been diverted. He stared longingly ahead.

"What's so interesting?" Joe asked.

"Don't pass it," pleaded Chet.

"Pass *what?*"

"That milk bar up there. They serve a terrific sundae, covered with whipped cream, cherries, and nuts. It's called a Bigloo Igloo. Come on, fellows. It's lunchtime."

"Okay." Frank laughed.

The yellow convertible turned in and stopped before the little white building. Soon the boys were seated together in a booth.

"Four Bigloo Igloos," ordered Chet, when the waitress came over.

"But there are only three of you, sir," the waitress protested.

"Four sundaes, miss," Chet repeated grandly. "Never fear—we shall dispose of them!"

The waitress shrugged and went off. The place was filled with people on their lunch hour, and there was a lively hubbub. A juke box was playing continuously. Suddenly, through the noise, Frank heard a voice behind him say:

". . . it will happen while the clock ticks."

The youth abruptly stood up, whirling, for a look at the speaker. His foot swung out into the aisle, tripping the waitress, who was returning with the boys' order!

Crash! Down went the girl. Up went four enormous Bigloo Igloo sundaes. Chet Morton stared aghast as two of them came down on his head. The others had found resting places on the floor.

Above the shrieks of the waitress, and the roars of laughter from the other customers, Frank cried, "Joe! Those two men who just went out— we must catch them!"

Pushing through the clogged aisle, the brothers paid the disconcerted waitress, then emerged from the milk bar in time to see a black car carrying two men speed away in the direction of Bayport.

"The fellow driving was tall—looked a lot like

Dalrymple!" called Frank as he sprinted for the convertible.

Joe followed, hurrying Chet, head still streaked with ice cream, along in front of him. They climbed into their car and gave chase.

The convertible slewed into the road with a squeal of rubber on concrete. By this time the other car was only a black dot on the highway ahead. Grimly, Frank pressed the accelerator to the floor.

"If it's the Meteor Special, you'll never catch it," Chet grumbled.

"That car wasn't a Meteor," Frank told him.

The highway rose, dipped, and turned. Sometimes the black dot was visible, sometimes not. Then, with a long straightaway in sight, it seemed to have disappeared altogether.

"They've ducked into the Willow River Road!" Frank guessed.

In a moment he made the turn himself, and raced along the familiar route. At the Purdy estate the gate was closed, and no car stood inside. Frank went on. He reached Shore Road without seeing a sign of the strange car.

"Lost them," Frank muttered in disgust.

Joe, too, frowned dejectedly. "Well, we may as well go see Mr. Applegate at Tower Mansion," he suggested. "It's right on this road."

The boys continued driving for some distance

until finally they glimpsed an immense stone structure high on a hill, overlooking the bay. The palatial building had the appearance of a feudal castle because of the two huge stone towers which arose from the far ends of it. Joe and Frank never failed to be impressed by the enormity of the old Tower Mansion and its well-kept, fence-enclosed grounds whenever their car climbed the wide driveway that led to the front entrance.

The elderly Mr. Applegate looked sad as he opened the door, yet he seemed glad to see the Hardys and their friend. He invited them into his living room.

"Boys," the old man said, "you helped me when my stamps were stolen, and I would have been lost without you the other night. If you can possibly get back my jade, I'll see that you're rewarded."

"You mean you want us to take the case, Mr. Applegate?" Joe asked.

"*You* can find my jade collection, if anybody can!" the elderly man declared firmly.

Suddenly Joe, Chet, and Hurd Applegate stared at Frank Hardy in astonishment. He had risen quietly from his chair and was tiptoeing stealthily toward the side window!

"What—what is it?" Chet gasped.

"Somebody in the yard—listening to us!" Frank whispered. With that, he raced through the house toward the rear door.

CHAPTER XIV

Sudden Attack

As FRANK burst from the back door, a man hurdled the hedge at the end of the Applegates' garden and sprinted through the rear of the property. The eavesdropper's tan sports jacket flapped behind him as he ran. He scaled the iron picket fence with the agility of a monkey and dropped to the roadway beyond. The man glanced backward, and Frank saw that he was heavily bearded.

"Up we go, fellows!" Frank urged.

In seconds the young sleuth, too, had cleared the fence. Behind him came Joe's pounding footsteps. Chet Morton, panting audibly, brought up the rear. They, too, scaled the fence.

Frank was looking up and down the roadway, puzzled. His quarry was no longer in sight. A young man wearing a striped blue jacket stood on the opposite side of the road, staring at two large, newly constructed houses.

Instantly Frank called to him. "Hey! Seen a man with a beard?"

"Right there . . . between those houses." The young man pointed. "Was he running away from you?"

Frank and his companions did not reply, but raced on between the houses. Still no sign of the stranger. The boys were in the midst of a housing development.

While Frank hurried forward to inspect the next street, Joe and Chet searched every possible hiding place in the yards. But it was no use. The boys had lost the eavesdropper completely.

"Bad break for us," Joe grumbled.

As the breathless trio retraced their steps, they noticed that the stranger in the blue jacket had disappeared. "Do you suppose he was telling the truth?" Chet asked. The Hardys shrugged.

Hurd Applegate was waiting for them on his back porch. "No luck, Mr. Applegate," said Joe to the old collector. "But we'll take your case. We'll find the stolen jade!"

Ten o'clock the next morning found the Hardy boys on the sidewalks of downtown Bayport. They were on their way to police headquarters to check on any new developments in the harbor mystery.

It was a hot, sunny day. Already the stores were lowering awnings over their display windows.

"Frank, look!" Joe pointed to a tall figure in a straw hat. His back was turned as he inspected the contents of a store window across the street. "It's Dalrymple. Wonder what's he doing in town?"

"We'd better speak to him," responded Frank. "He might be on his way to the Purdy place in spite of our warning."

Crossing at the corner, the boys went up and touched their client's shoulder. As the man whirled, Frank and Joe stepped back in surprise. He was not Mr. Dalrymple!

"What d'you want?" the stranger demanded roughly.

"You're the man who stole Hurd Applegate's jade!" Joe fearlessly accused him.

"What jade? I don't know what you're talking about. I never saw you before! You watch your tongue. I could sue you!"

Shoving past the boys, he darted around some pedestrians and threw himself into the front seat of a black car parked at the curb. At that moment the light changed to green. The stranger's automobile was sucked into a river of traffic which surged forward until the light changed.

"Why did we let him go?" Joe stormed.

"We could be wrong," Frank told his brother. "Anyway, I got the license number. We'll give it to Chief Collig."

"It wasn't a Meteor Special," Joe noted.

"Maybe that's the car we chased yesterday!"

Eagerly the boys hurried to headquarters.

"So you think you may have seen the thief!" Collig exclaimed. "Your friend Dalrymple just called. He doesn't believe such a man as his double exists."

"He exists all right," answered Frank. "Here's the number of the car he was driving."

Immediately the resources of a modern police department were brought into play. The strange car was found to be registered in the name of James Black of Bayport. When questioned on the telephone, Mr. Black said he was about to call the police himself—to report that his car had been stolen!

"Better come down and tell us about it, Mr. Black," said the officer into the phone. Within half an hour a well-dressed, slight, middle-aged man was escorted by a patrolman into the chief's office. Frank and Joe, meanwhile, had concealed themselves in an adjoining room.

"Tell us about your car, Mr. Black," the chief began. "Where do you keep it?"

"Why . . . in my garage."

Frank and Joe noted that, while facing the chief, the man kept averting his eyes.

"Mighty bold thief, to take your car from your garage," Chief Collig remarked.

"As a matter of fact, it was parked at the curb in front of the house."

"When? Last night?"

"Yes—that's it—last night."

"So, Mr. Black, your car was stolen sometime last night. Must have upset you!"

"Yes," the man stammered. "I—I've been a nervous wreck ever since I discovered it was gone —right after I got up this morning."

"Of course. What time do you get up?"

"About seven."

"And you noticed the car was gone then?" pursued the chief. "It was ten-thirty when I called you, Mr. Black. You say you were upset about your car being stolen, yet you let three hours go by before reporting it to the police!"

For a moment James Black blinked in silence, obviously disconcerted.

"Here, you can't browbeat me this way," he blustered. "I—I just didn't realize my car was actually stolen, that's all. You act like you're trying to accuse *me* of a crime!"

"If you ask me, Mr. Black, *you* act like a man who's been accused of a crime."

"Well, you haven't anything on me," the stranger snapped suddenly. "I don't have a record. You can't hold me without charges."

"Charges?" said Collig politely. "I thought you came to make a complaint, Mr. Black. Now that you've made it, you may as well go."

As soon as the man had left, Frank and Joe stepped into the office.

"That guy might be on the level," declared Joe. "But he sure doesn't give me that impression."

Chief Collig nodded agreement. "We'll watch him," he promised. "Best way to catch a crook is to make him believe you've decided he's innocent."

When the brothers reached home, Aunt Gertrude was on the phone talking with Chet. "Here they come now," she said. "But no sleuthing this afternoon. Our grass is high enough to turn a herd of cows into, and the flower beds are full of weeds. Frank and Joe aren't going off this property until the place looks respectable again."

As Miss Hardy turned the phone over to Frank, she gave him a look which plainly meant, "No arguments!"

For this reason dusk was falling before the two detectives were free to leave. As the street lights winked on, a ten-year-old car pulled up in front of the Hardys' house. Flashlights in hand, Frank and Joe came down to join Chet Morton, who sat at the car's wheel.

"Where to?" he asked.

"Tonight we try out the third key on the chain the jeweler gave us," Frank replied as they drove off. "My guess is that it fits the front door in the Purdy homestead."

It was totally dark when the friends concealed Chet's car a distance down Willow River Road, and walked to the Purdy grounds. They crept stealthily along the wall. Finding the gate unlocked, they slipped through it.

The old mansion looked up, solid and dark, against a star-filled sky. The moon had not yet risen. Silently Frank tiptoed up the front steps and tried the key.

"Doesn't fit," he whispered, rejoining the other boys. "Wish Dalrymple hadn't forgotten the spare set of keys."

The three slipped around to the back door. But again the key would not fit.

"Cellar door," suggested Joe, feeling his way to the bulkhead nearby.

Frank inserted the key. "It works!" he whispered excitedly. "The fellow must keep the front-door key separate."

Silently he and Joe raised the heavy doors. Frank pocketed the key, and the three cautiously went down the steps into the blackness below.

The boys dared not use their flashlights, lest the beams be seen through the chinks in the flooring overhead. Frank and Joe led the way across the dank, musty cellar. Chet, shuddering a bit, followed as closely as possible. Suddenly the plump boy gave a choked cry and sprang sideways.

Crash—clatter!

Silence. At once the Hardys turned on their flashlights. In the circle of light was Chet, lying half underneath a jumble of wooden boxes.

In a hoarse, terrified voice he gasped, "S-s-some-thing alive ran over m-my feet!" Frank looked about quickly. Then he pointed. "There it is—in the corner. A rat!"

Even as he spoke, the creature scurried out of sight. Chet, a bit shaken, was hauled to his feet, and the three advanced toward a stairway.

"Wait!" Frank commanded. "Someone's up-stairs!"

There were the sound of voices and the creak-ing of floor boards above them.

"The—thieves?" Chet gulped.

Joe started up the steps. "Let's find out!" he said grimly.

The three boys found the door at the top of the stairs locked.

"All right," Frank whispered. "If we can't get in, we'll get them out. Make all the racket you can. We'll nab whoever comes out."

Instantly the three boys pounded on the door, hammered the walls, shouted, and stamped on the steps. In a minute, above the pandemonium, came loud voices from inside.

"Hey! What's goin' on? Cops! A raid! Beat it!" Heavy footsteps tore through the house.

Still shouting, the three youths clattered down the steps and dashed across the cellar. As they emerged from the bulkhead, two black forms leaped from a window and made for the river.

Two black forms leaped from a window and made
for the river

"Come on!" cried Joe. "We've got 'em now!"

Pell-mell the brothers raced into the woods and onto the path. Chet followed as best he could. At the river the Hardys found a big, empty motorboat floating on the dark surface.

"The men are still around here," said Frank tensely. "I—"

He never finished the sentence. The brothers were grabbed from behind by powerful arms and knocked to the ground. Their flashlights flew from their hands. A moment later Frank and Joe were gagged and bound tightly. Then they were dragged off and tumbled into the boat.

There was the sound of a man grunting. Then the motor whirred, caught, and roared.

The boat moved out on the water. Joe and Frank saw the black, receding shore on their right, and realized they were heading upriver. The brothers hoped fervently that Chet had escaped. The outlines of their captors rose above the prostrate boys. Against the stars they saw that one was tall. The other, at the tiller, was broad and husky, with a huge jutting jaw.

"The man who drove the limousine!" Joe told himself.

"What'll we do with 'em?" muttered the tall man, crouching down.

Frank and Joe waited with pounding hearts for a reply. It came.

"Dump 'em overboard!"

CHAPTER XV

The Vanishing Car

To Frank and Joe, lying bound in an inch of water at the bottom of the boat, it seemed they had been speeding up the dark river for hours. The boys' arms and fingers were numb where the coarse ropes bit into their flesh, cutting off circulation. The tall man sat guard over them on a middle seat. At long intervals he would argue with the tough, large-jawed man steering the boat.

"We'd be crazy to dump these kids, Sid," he muttered. "Kidnaping's bad enough—it's a Federal offense."

"Shut up, Benny. You're yellow," sneered his companion. "We'll sink 'em right along here somewhere. Get the sea anchor ready. That'll do it."

A chill went through the Hardys. Joe's head

was jammed between the side of the boat and the middle seat. Frantically he rubbed his head against both, hoping to loosen his gag.

"I tell ya I won't have any part of it!" said Benny.

"Don't then. I'll do it myself!"

The muscular crook throttled down and stood up to move forward. Just as he did, Joe finally worked his gag loose.

"Help!" he shouted. *"Help! Quick!"*

As the two thieves advanced on the boy, powerful lights flashed on along shore. The full-throated roar of a big launch was heard. A siren wailed, and the motorboat was caught in the long beam of a spotlight.

Instantly the heavily built man leaped back to the stern and jammed his throttle wide open. The boat raced into the darkness.

"That won't save you," yelled Joe, fearful that the two desperate men might throw their captives overboard to slow up their pursuers. "The police have stations all along this river. You're as good as caught."

In answer, the big-jawed driver slammed the tiller from side to side. The craft lunged crazily, trying to escape the search beam.

"You'll wreck us!" screamed the tall man in terror.

"Yes—just like you two wrecked the *Napoli* in the bay," cried Joe on a sudden hunch. "You don't know this river any more than you knew the harbor. It's night and you're running without lights. The water's deep here. You won't get out of *this* wreck alive!"

"He's right—we haven't a chance, Sid," the tall man pleaded. "Stop her!"

There was a quick warning burst of machine-gun fire. Muttering, Sid killed his motor. A white glare bathed the whole boat. The heavy hull of the police launch drew alongside, and a stout figure jumped into the thieves' craft.

"Chet!" Joe cried joyously.

"You're here—and safe!" Chet cried out in relief. Quickly he freed his two chums, while their captors were handcuffed by two officers and taken aboard the launch.

As the launch turned and headed for Bayport, the Hardys leaned back in relief. Frank said, "Good work, Chet. You and the police got here just in time!"

"I saw those toughs jump you and start upriver," the plump boy explained. "I ran like mad for the car and raced to the police substation up here. They radioed for a launch. Soon as it arrived, I got on. We started checking all boats and docks. Then we heard you yell, Joe."

"Lucky for us, partner," Frank declared gratefully, rubbing his wrists.

The police launch docked briefly at the upriver substation.

"You boys pick up your car here," said the commander of the boat. "We'll meet you at Bayport headquarters with these two customers."

After a bracing cup of hot broth at the substation, Frank, Joe, and Chet left for Bayport in Chet's car. At police headquarters they found Chief Collig and the officers with him thwarted by the thugs' refusal to admit anything.

"We don't know nothin' about any waterfront robberies," Sid snarled. "You got evidence? You can't touch us without evidence!"

"We'll charge you with kidnaping!" snapped Chief Collig. "That'll do for a start."

The man called Benny looked uncertain, but his accomplice taunted, "Yeah? That won't tell you what you want to know."

At this point Frank spoke up. "Chief, I have a strong hunch there's evidence at the Purdy place. Let Chet, Joe, and me get it!"

"Good idea," agreed the chief. "Tomlin, take a prowl car and go with them."

For the second time that night the friends drove out to the old house. On this visit they rode up to the house, following Officer Tomlin, and let themselves in through the open window from which the thugs had escaped.

Soon lights were blazing in every room of the old mansion as the three boys and the policeman went from room to room, searching.

"Look here!" Chet yelled, as he pulled open

the door of a corner cupboard in the dining room and revealed a number of cardboard cartons.

Tomlin and the Hardys lifted them down and opened one. It proved to contain carefully wrapped pieces of solid silver imprinted with a foreign hallmark.

"It's part of the stolen loot, all right," Tomlin pronounced. "But it wasn't here the last time we searched."

Eagerly the four peered into the other boxes, and found an assortment of fine china, expensive jewelry, and a diamond ring and gold articles which matched the description of the crewman's missing valuables.

Joe frowned. "I don't see Hurd Applegate's collection or Captain Stroman's jade necklace."

Again the searchers went to work. They examined the third floor, the attic, and the cellar, but found nothing more.

"This is enough evidence to confront those two crooks with, anyhow," said Tomlin finally. "They must've stowed the stuff here right after the chief's search. I'll run it in now."

"Right," Frank agreed. "We'll follow you as soon as we pick up our flashlights. We lost them on the riverbank."

They retrieved the two flashlights at the foot of the river path. The three boys passed the big house, now dark and silent once more, and walked down the driveway.

"That place gives me the willies," muttered Chet, as Frank closed the gate. "I still have the creepy feeling that somebody's in there, watching everything that goes on."

They reached Chet's car and piled in. While Chet was digging for his keys, the boys heard the roar of an approaching automobile. The vehicle raced toward them without lights, veered sharply, and sped up to the Purdy gate. The driver leaped out, yanked open the gate, jumped back into the car, and drove through.

"After him!" urged Joe.

In a moment Chet had his ancient motor running and his headlights on. He made a quick U-turn and sped in pursuit through the gate, up the driveway to the house, and around to the other side where the road apparently ended.

Quickly the boys jumped out. Before them was the dense brush which covered most of the estate. Saplings, heavily draped with leafy vines, rose up like a wall in the glare of the headlights.

Frank got down and examined the ground. "Tire tracks leading straight into the brush," he reported, puzzled.

Joe impulsively stepped up to the leafy wall. He grasped a hanging vine and pulled hard. The whole green tangle slid along a tree branch, like a drapery!

"A hidden road!" declared Chet in wonder.

He turned out the lights of his car. Then, cautiously, the three set out on foot along the mysterious road.

At intervals they could make out bits of sky through the leaves overhead. They halted abruptly when something black and solid loomed up ahead of them. After listening carefully and hearing nothing, Frank risked the use of his flashlight.

In its beam they saw a small tumble-down barn with a gaping doorway. Frank stooped to examine the ground. Tire tracks led straight to the dilapidated building!

Joe flicked on his flashlight and the three boys stepped warily inside the barn. The front of the old structure was empty to the roof, but in the far half of the barn was an old haymow.

The front beam supporting the loft was sagging, and the dusty hay, closely matted together, spilled forward over it like a stationary waterfall. The cascade of hay formed a curtain reaching almost to the floor of the barn.

"Boy!" said Chet. "Bet that hay's been here since Jason Purdy died."

"Then why is this pitchfork so new?" Joe pointed to a tool nearby with three slender steel tines, and a clean-grained wooden handle.

"And where's that car?" asked Frank.

He had a sudden inspiration. Frank pushed his arms through the hanging of old hay. His knuckles rapped wood. Tearing the hay aside, the boy laid bare a broad sheet of plywood with a handle.

Eagerly Frank grasped the handle. A door rolled smoothly open.

Joe and Chet gasped. There, in a secret garage underneath the hayloft, was the back end of a late-model Meteor Special!

Frank already had penetrated to the other end of the garage. "Motor's still hot," he called back. "She must have just been driven in."

Chet and Joe rushed over. "I get it," said Joe. "After the car's in, they pull down some more hay from the loft to hide the plywood. That's what the pitchfork is for."

"*Sh!*" Chet put a warning finger to his lips. "Hear something? A kind of moaning?"

Frank played his light around the garage. Nothing. He shone the flash into the back seat of the Meteor Special.

"Good night!" he exclaimed, staring.

On the floor of the car a man lay bound and gagged.

CHAPTER XVI

A Missing Client

CHET gulped. "S-somebody got him, too!" While he and Joe held the flashlights, Frank reached into the car and cut the groaning man's bonds. Slowly and painfully he clambered out, smoothing his rumpled clothes.

"Say!" Joe cried. "We've seen you before!"

He was the young man in the striped blue jacket they had encountered while chasing the eavesdropper. At this moment, instead of being grateful for the rescue, the man glared angrily. He pulled out a handkerchief to mop his glistening forehead. As he did, something fell to the ground.

Joe recognized the object instantly and scooped it up. "A false beard!"

"*You* were the one listening under Hurd Applegate's window!" Frank accused the stranger. "Okay. Now spill it! Why the disguise—what's your game?"

The Hardys gripped the man's arms. His angry manner changed to one of sullen defeat. "All right, all right. Let go of me," he muttered. "So I *was* the eavesdropper. A fat lot of good it did me! Even this jacket didn't help except once." He pulled open the jacket. "See? Tan on the inside. When you guys came after me I just reversed it and took off my beard."

"And sent us on a false trail," Joe scowled. "Keep talking!"

"I'm a private detective—at least, I *thought* I was. After this, I feel like giving up the business!"

Frank's mind raced. "Private detective, eh? *You're* the 'Mr. Smith' who questioned our Aunt Gertrude!"

The young man nodded. "Sam Allen is my real name. I'm supposed to find out about Captain Stroman's stolen necklace. I heard you'd been to see him—that's why I was checking on you. Well, I learned old Applegate had lost some jade, too. That big guy with the glasses—Arthur Jensen—was the one who took 'em. That much I found out."

"Arthur Jensen?" repeated Frank, exchanging glances with Joe. It was the first time the Hardys had heard the name. But each wondered if Jensen and Mr. Dalrymple's double were the same man.

"Yeah. I've been tailing him all over town," Allen went on. "Finally I hid under a rug in the back seat of his car. I thought he'd lead me to

Stroman's necklace. Then I sneezed. Next thing, Jensen conked me and I was out like a light. When I came to, there I was all trussed up, with a lump on my head. Some detective!"

"Nobody's perfect." Frank smiled, satisfied that Sam Allen was telling the truth. "Let's combine forces and search the estate for Jensen."

Allen brightened. "You bet!"

The three boys and the humbled "private eye" entered the Purdy house through the still-open window, and made a thorough, but unsuccessful, search of the interior.

"He could be hiding anywhere in the underbrush," Frank observed as they left the house. "We probably wouldn't find him tonight. I suggest we report this to headquarters."

The four drove back to town in Chet's car.

"You can let me off at my motel," Sam Allen told them. "I've had all the detective work I can stand for one night."

Frank, Joe, and Chet headed for police headquarters. They found Chief Collig and his officers considerably more cheerful. The two thugs, Benny and Sid, sat uncomfortably on straight chairs in Collig's office. A police clerk was taking notes rapidly in shorthand.

"These birds have been singing ever since I brought in the loot we found," Officer Tomlin told the Hardys in an undertone. "The husky one is Sid Bowler. The string bean is Benny Vance."

The boys took seats and listened intently.

"Yeah, we used to 'borrow' motorboats," Bowler was saying. "We used 'em to see if the coast was clear, and then to steal from the ships."

"Steal what?" Collig prodded.

"Everything."

"Including jade?" Frank Hardy suddenly broke in.

Bowler gave him a baleful glare. "Jade, too."

"Who's your leader?" Joe demanded.

"There ain't any leader," was the sullen answer. "There's just me and Benny."

"You mean you and Benny stole thousands of dollars' worth of jade and other stuff on your own?" Joe snorted. "What a laugh! We know all about your big boss—Jensen."

The two prisoners almost jumped from their chairs. "H-how did you find—" Benny began.

Sid turned on him. "You fool! *Shut up!*"

As Benny slumped in his seat, Frank pressed, "No use denying it, Bowler. Now, where's Jensen —and the jade?"

"Find out yourself," Bowler muttered. "If you do, you can pin the whole idea on Jensen."

Chief Collig and his men were looking at the Hardys in amazement. The chief signaled them to continue questioning, if they wished.

Joe nodded. "What were you doing in the boat the night I chased you and Bowler?" he demanded of Benny Vance.

"We—we were looking for a chance to get on board the *Sea Bright* again that night and steal some stuff we'd missed."

"Stuff you missed when you borrowed the *Sleuth?*"

"Yes. It was a double job, see," Benny Vance explained, evidently eager to co-operate. "We stole Stroman's jade necklace and old Applegate's collection, too. Sid and I robbed the *Sea Bright,* Jensen and Black went to Applegate's."

"So Black's in your gang?" Joe interrupted.

"Sure. Jensen went in and got Applegate to show him some of his best jade. Then he ran off with it, see? The old man chased him, and left his house empty."

Sid Bowler put in with disgust, "That's when Black was supposed to sneak in and get the rest. But he chickened out, so Jensen went back and got it just before you guys brought Applegate home. Black was supposed to meet us at the docks, but never showed. We had your blue-and-white boat ready to take him upriver to the Purdy place."

Joe nodded. "And you met Jensen out there. He had the jade and you had the other loot."

"Yeah."

"Whose idea was it to start using privately owned boats?" Chief Collig asked the prisoners.

"Jensen's," Vance replied. "Soon as the cops started patrolling the roads, he had us 'borrow' different boats so we couldn't be identified and the owners would be suspected." The thief shook his head. "Things were getting hot, with the cops and these Hardy pests here. When we heard 'em in the cellar tonight we thought for sure it was a raid."

On Chief Collig's orders, Bowler and Vance were led back to their cells. Then the officer turned to the boys and grinned. "Bring me up to date. How'd you unearth all this about Jensen?"

While the chief and other officers listened in astonishment, the Hardys poured out the story of the hidden garage and private detective Sam Allen. Frank handed over the ignition key.

"This practically wraps up the case!" declared Chief Collig enthusiastically. Rapidly he issued orders to one of his captains:

"Take every man available. Wait till daylight, and then search the house and grounds with a fine-tooth comb for Jensen and Black and the loot! Bring in the black Meteor when you come back.

"But in case those two thieves have already skipped town," the chief turned to another officer, "I want a dragnet out beyond Bayport. Contact the county sheriff patrols and state police. We'll send out an interstate alarm for these men."

After the policemen had hurried off to carry out orders, Frank, Joe, and Chet were left alone with their old friend.

"You boys have done a job Fenton Hardy will be proud of," Chief Collig told them. "Go home and get a good night's sleep. By tomorrow we'll have this case wrapped up. Check with me tomorrow afternoon."

The chief then proposed assigning a twenty-four-hour police guard at the Purdy place. The Hardys felt that this might hamper them in solving Mr. Dalrymple's mystery.

"It may keep the crooks from returning," Frank said quietly.

"True. I'll let the place appear to be deserted," Collig agreed. As the friends drove home through the quiet streets of the sleeping city, both Frank and Joe expressed misgivings.

"I don't know," said Frank, troubled. "Jensen and Black are still on the loose. And we don't know where the jade is."

"Also," Joe reminded him, "the notes threatening Mr. Dalrymple haven't been explained, or that weird scream we heard from the Purdy house the first night we went there."

"Yes," mused Joe. "I have a feeling this case is a long way from closed."

"Some sleep will help," grumbled Chet, yawning.

Early the next morning Frank telephoned to Mr. Dalrymple's home in Lakeside. He wanted to report the previous night's events at the old house, and also let him know about the cellar key.

Receiving no answer, he called their client's bank.

"Sorry, sir. Mr. Dalrymple hasn't come in this morning. No one here knows where he is."

All morning the two brothers remained at home, calling Lakeside at intervals. Shortly after lunch they drove down to police headquarters.

There they found Chief Collig weary from lack of sleep, and much less optimistic than he had been the previous night. He said Black had been picked up in a motel in another town. He was being brought to Bayport.

"We went over every inch of the Purdy place," the chief complained. "Got the Meteor, but not a trace of Jensen, nor of the loot, either. The gang must have it hidden some place else. As for Jensen, we can only hope our dragnet will work."

After the brothers left headquarters, Frank stepped into a public telephone booth to make another call to Dalrymple's home. No answer. Then he tried the bank again. An assistant reported:

"Sorry, sir. Nobody has heard from him yet."

"I don't like it," Frank told his brother with a frown. "We'd better get over to Lakeside."

By late afternoon the Hardys' yellow convertible was parked in front of the banker's residence in the nearby city. But their knocks and calls went unanswered. All the doors were locked.

"We'd better get the police," Frank said gravely, as he and Joe drove off.

Half an hour later the young detectives re-turned with a squad of policemen. "We suspect something's happened to Mr. Dalrymple," Frank told the sergeant in charge. "You'd better search the place."

Two big policemen quickly forced the door. The handsome rooms of the house were in perfect order. There was no sign of Mr. Dalrymple.

The police sergeant promised to notify the boys of any new developments, then he and his men left. The Hardys somberly climbed into their own car. As they drove off, Frank confessed his worst fears. "I'm afraid Mr. Dalrymple's been decoyed to the Purdy place, and is in danger. We'd better head for there."

By now it was early evening. The Hardys' car raced through the countryside. Storm clouds were piling up in the west. Suddenly, without warning, the car's engine coughed and died.

In disgust, the Hardys got out and pushed the convertible to the side of the road. When a quick examination failed to locate the trouble, Frank said, "We can't wait. We'll have to walk."

Dusk came on rapidly, as the two boys hurried along the highway. An hour's hike brought them to the Willow Road turnoff. Finally they reached the darkened Purdy mansion. No police stopped them, nor were any in sight. Frank and Joe went to the cellar entrance.

"Lucky we have this key, anyhow," said Frank.

Thunder rumbled in the black sky above as he unlocked the bulkhead. To their surprise, the brothers found the door to the kitchen unlocked. They opened it and tiptoed inside.

As the Hardys moved forward in the darkness into the living room, they were suddenly seized and thrown to the floor by someone of enormous strength. Though weary from their long walk, the boys fought back, but were overpowered by blows on the head. Frank, semiconscious, was dragged across the floor, shoved into a chair, and bound to it. A piece of cloth was tied tightly over his mouth. Then the sounds of struggling near him ceased. Joe too had been over-powered. There was silence, broken by a single repetitious:

Tick-tock. Tick-tock. Tick-tock.

There was something ominous about the steady, measured sound. Frank, still half dazed, wondered if his brother was in the same room, or had been taken to another part of the house.

Suddenly Frank became aware of stealthy foot-steps approaching and heavy breathing. The boy felt the hairs on his scalp stiffen as he sensed the presence of someone next to his chair.

Was the person the boys' attacker? Frank seethed with chagrin at being unable to defend himself. He tensed, expecting the worst.

CHAPTER XVII

A Dangerous Ticking

FRANK HARDY's spine tingled as he waited for the unknown person's first move. Then from the darkness came a gloating voice.

"So, we have trapped the young snoopers! How fortunate that we were ready for your arrival!"

Suddenly a low light was turned on, illuminating the living room. In a flash, Frank took in the whole scene. The old draperies had been drawn shut.

There was the immense grandfather's clock in the corner. Nearby was his brother Joe, tightly lashed, like himself, to an old-fashioned high-backed chair. Confronting both boys was a tall, rather heavy-set man wearing glasses.

The brothers recognized him instantly—the person who resembled Mr. Dalrymple. He introduced himself as Arthur Jensen, ringleader of the harbor thieves!

"He must be the one who clobbered us when we came in," Joe told himself. "The sneak!"

Now the man looked from one of his captives to the other. "Surprised you, didn't I? Ha! That'll teach you to meddle in other people's business!"

Joe felt a sudden surge of anger. "Business!" he exclaimed to himself. "If we ever get out of this mess, I'll show him!"

Meanwhile, Jensen went on triumphantly, "Yes, my young sleuths, we have many more surprises for you this evening. Your friend Dalrymple will be surprised, too. And, I might add, my resemblance to him has come in very handy."

He gazed at the brothers mockingly. "You Hardys thought you were so bright. Yet you never dreamed that every time you and the police came in here, we were watching you."

Although Frank and Joe gave no visible indication of fear, both realized that they were at the mercy of a clever, unscrupulous gangster. In spite of their predicament, however, the boys wondered who else had been "watching" them with Jensen, and from what point in the house.

Just then there came a squeaky noise from the direction of the clock. Jensen whirled around.

"Oh, Amos!" he called. "Come on out. We have visitors."

While Frank and Joe stared in utter amaze-

ment, the huge clock and the wall section behind
it began sliding to one side.

"Why," Frank gave an inward gasp, "it's a door,
hidden by the clock attached to it!"

In another moment there emerged from the
opening a gaunt, white-haired old man. He was
clean shaven, and had kind blue eyes. He started
forward, then stopped upon noticing the two
boys.

"Mr. Jensen," he said uncertainly, "these
young men—visitors? But why are they bound up
in this fashion?"

Frank and Joe exchanged puzzled glances. Was
this gentle-mannered, elderly man connected with
Jensen's racket? Somehow, he did not seem the
type, they thought.

"You'll understand in due time, Amos," the
gangster leader said with a sneer. Then, noticing
the Hardys' curious looks at the old man, Jensen
added with mock courtesy, "Oh, excuse me. You
haven't been introduced. This, boys, is Mr. Amos
Wandy, an inventor. Very clever, too. Amos, these
young men are the Hardy brothers."

Mr. Wandy nodded slowly. "Yes, I remember
having seen them here. You said they were out to
wreck your project. But really, they seem like
harmless lads. I don't think—"

"Never mind what you think!" Jensen told the
old inventor in a ruthless tone. "Have you finished your job?"

"Yes, yes, I have." Amos Wandy looked at Jensen with a perplexed expression. "It's finished. No need to get excited."

"Who's excited!" snapped Jensen. "Bring that gadget out here!"

Mr. Wandy hastened through the opened wall section. Arthur Jensen turned to the Hardys. "One of the surprises I mentioned," he told them with a leer. "Even you didn't figure there might be *two* secret rooms here, did you? Or that I was sitting behind the clock while you or the police snooped around. Only this morning I waited in there, while half the Bayport force inspected the place."

Silently Frank berated himself. "Why didn't I think there might be a hiding place behind that clock! Especially after those threatening notes to Mr. Dalrymple."

In the meantime, Joe was trying to make sense of what was taking place. Was Arthur Jensen the one who had sent the threatening notes to Dalrymple? And was Wandy in league with him? Joe could not imagine the elderly inventor causing anyone harm.

At that moment Amos Wandy reappeared, gingerly carrying a heavy object that looked like a black box, except that it had a number of electrical terminals on one side.

"Ah, good!" declared Jensen, rubbing his

hands. "Know what this is?" he asked the Hardys, pointing to the black box.

Frank and Joe realized at once what the object was. *A time bomb!* The brothers felt a mounting apprehension.

"I see you *are* familiar with this type of apparatus," Jensen went on, chuckling. "Well, old Amos here knows all about bombs, too, don't you, Amos?"

The old man answered readily, "Yes, I told you that, Mr. Jensen. In the course of my work with electronically activated devices, I naturally—"

"Cut the fancy talk," the other man broke in roughly. "All I care about is whether that bomb you're holding has enough 'juice' in it to wipe this pile of bricks right off the map!"

A hideous wave of panic swept over the Hardys. "Does Jensen mean to blow us up?" Frank asked himself unbelievingly.

It was then that the boys noticed Amos Wandy's face. It had turned deathly pale. For a moment he swayed, as if about to faint. Then he clutched the deadly looking device tightly.

"What did you say, Mr. Jensen?" he quavered. "You told me this bomb was for some construction work. I—I don't understand—"

"You soon will, Amos," said the gang leader in a sinister voice. "Put down the bomb. I'll take over."

But the old inventor did not comply. He re-treated a few steps backward. "No, Mr. Jensen," he objected. "I fear you are going to use this for some other purpose. An evil purpose. What's more, you have lied to me about these boys—they are your prisoners. In fact, you've lied to me about everything—you never intended to help me market my new invention, as you promised!"

Without warning, Jensen made a lunge for the elderly man and ripped the box from his grasp. The next instant, he knocked the inventor to the floor with a sweep of his big arm. Amos Wandy lay still, stunned.

Jensen then put down the bomb and whipped from his pocket a length of rope. He bound the white-haired man's arms and legs securely.

"Yes, Amos," he taunted. "These boys *are* my prisoners. And now, so are you—you have been all along. Only you were so wrapped up in your precious invention you never suspected it. Lucky I found you here, and had you hoodwinked long enough to put this bomb together."

The big man straightened up and, his eyes burning strangely, went on, "Now all three of you will have the privilege of sharing the success of the explosive—at the proper time."

Amos Wandy had recovered sufficiently to mur-mur brokenly, "You—you're insane, Jensen. You—you can't get away with it."

"Can't I? You'll see. But I'd better shut you up before I get to work."

Jensen dashed from the room and was back with a piece of cloth with which he gagged Mr. Wandy.

"Now, I will proceed with my—er—operation." He gave an exaggerated sigh. "Too bad my pals got caught. I could sure use their help now."

The three silenced prisoners watched in growing horror as their captor took several wires from another pocket. He squatted down over the heavy black box. His fingers worked swiftly, attaching the wires to the terminals. He then moved the whole device closer to the clock and ran the wires up into the works.

"You see, Amos," he looked slyly over his shoulder, "I'm pretty good at this sort of thing myself."

Jensen stood up, smirking. Dramatically he pointed to the face of the huge timepiece and faced his captives.

"You will note the hour," he said. "I have arranged that when the hands of this clock reach three, the bomb will be set off!"

The Hardys stared at the clockface. It was already past one o'clock in the morning! For a second both boys were engulfed by a wave of panic. Through their minds flashed the words of the ominous notes:

"Death while the clock ticks!"

But their natural instinct of keeping cool in crises asserted itself. Frank and Joe furtively tried to move their wrists to loosen their bonds.

In the meantime, Jensen continued to talk, growing more pleased with himself by the minute. "You remember what you boys overheard in that restaurant?" he reminded them. "Of course, I didn't expect *you'd* be my guests—or that *you'd* found my key ring. But you've asked for it. You'll never interfere with me again after tonight. Nor will that pest Dalrymple."

"Dalrymple!" the name echoed through the boys' minds. What *had* happened to the banker? Was he too a captive somewhere in the shadowy old mansion?

All this while Frank, Joe, and Amos Wandy were acutely aware of the inexorable swinging of the clock's pendulum as the minutes ticked by.

Again the brothers wriggled their wrists and fingers in an effort to loosen the ropes. But the result was only to rub their skin raw. The bonds were cruelly tight.

If only, they thought desperately, someone would become anxious because of their long absence, and figure out where they were! "Aunt Gertrude must be frantic by now," Joe thought hopefully.

In the meantime, Arthur Jensen had been eying his prisoners smugly. "Well," he said, "I suppose you wonder how I came to discover the hidden room behind the clock, and how nicely it has served my purpose—thanks to Amos, here."

The gangster went on to explain that when he had first started to use the Purdy place to hide stolen valuables, he had come upon Mr. Wandy in the house.

"You see," Jensen went on, "Amos told me he was Jason Purdy's cousin. They played here as youngsters—that's how he came to know about both secret rooms. All these years he kept a key to the place. When he retired, old Amos still wanted to fool around with inventing, so he decided to come here and work on some gadgets. He thought nobody would bother him.

"Well, we met here by accident. I thought his talents would be useful to us, so I told him I'd help him get his inventions on the market when they were ready, if he'd do some work for us."

Jensen looked scornfully down at Mr. Wandy, whose blue eyes blazed with anger.

"So," the thief continued, "I set up the clock room as a lab—and also a storage place for our loot. Everything went smoothly until that Dalrymple guy came along and bought this place. It was a pain in the neck with his nosing around. That's why I left those notes in the secret room upstairs. Then he had to drag *you* kids here."

The man paused and a cunning gleam came

into his eyes. "Bet you boys would like to know *how* I got the notes in there. Well, that's something you'll never find out now!"

At least, Joe was thinking bitterly, Jensen was not getting away with most of the stolen goods. "He must have the jade stashed behind that clock section," the boy surmised.

"No doubt you'd like to know about that scream you heard one night. Well, I did that—pretty effective, wasn't it? Sure scared the wits out of that old fool who came after me. Serves him right."

"He means Hurd Applegate," Frank thought, thinking wryly that not only were he and Joe unable to help themselves, but in their present state were of no use to Applegate or Dalrymple. "Wonder how Dad would get out of such a mess!"

At this point Jensen ceased his narrative and glanced at the big clock. The hands stood at quarter past two.

"Well," he said briskly, "time is fleeting. I'm going to get out of here but fast."

He hastened to the hidden room behind the clock. The Hardys could hear muffled thumping, as if Jensen were moving cartons. Finally he reappeared, with a heavy canvas sack slung over his shoulder and an armload of small boxes.

Suddenly they all became aware of vivid flashes of lightning, followed by the deafening boom of thunder. Then came a torrential downpour of rain. "Storm's hit," Jensen said. He added meaningfully, "But it's nothing compared to what you'll see at three o'clock!"

He gave a triumphant laugh when he noticed the Hardys staring at his bag and boxes. "Oh, yes," he went on, "you didn't think I'd leave all this precious jade behind! Not after the trouble I went through to get it. The police can keep that other stuff!"

Jensen's eyes swept the room, and came to rest on the three bound and gagged figures. "I've enjoyed your visit." He laughed again. "I'll leave the light on so you can watch the time. Good-by!"

He left the room. In another moment the boys heard the front door open, then slam shut.

Almost automatically, the three captives turned their gaze toward the grandfather's clock.

"A quarter to three!" Joe's mouth felt parched and beads of sweat broke out on his forehead.

He and Frank and Amos Wandy could only wait and listen to the deadly sound of the clock.

Tick-tock. Tick-tock. Tick-tock.

CHAPTER XVIII

The Slippery Rooftop

"THE fiend!" Frank gritted his teeth. "Jensen's really left us here to be blown sky-high!"

Desperately he strained his arms and legs against the rough ropes that cut into his flesh. It was to no avail. Then he lurched forward, trying to overturn the chair with the thought of working himself across the floor toward the time bomb. This attempt proved futile, too.

Joe, meanwhile, was squirming and twisting his body in an effort to get his penknife. But his fingers would reach no farther than the edge of his pocket.

Old Amos Wandy lay still, as if resigned to their horrible fate. The clock ticked on relentlessly. With a shudder the Hardys noted the time.

Five minutes before three!

The boys sank back, exhausted from their struggles. Only a miracle could save them now!

A tremendous crashing of thunder shook the entire house. As it died away, Joe stared in fascination at the big front window. Strangely, one of the panes continued to rattle. Was it his imagination or did he see a face pressed against the streaming glass where the draperies had parted a little?

Joe squinted his eyes, hardly daring to believe them. There *was* a face peering in—a familiar one!

Chet Morton!

Frank had seen him, too. The brothers looked at the clock. Less than two minutes left!

"Please, Chet!" Frank begged silently. "Get in here!"

The stout boy did not hesitate. He pushed with all his weight upward against the sash. The window flew up. Chet clambered over the sill.

In seconds, his sharp jackknife had sliced through Frank's ropes. Without a word Frank dived forward, seized the wires running from the black bomb to the clock, and tore them away.

For a moment he stared at the wires, lying tangled on the floor. Before either Chet or Frank could say anything, the clock struck. *Bong! Bong! Bong!*

"Three o'clock!" Frank gasped, weak with relief. "Chet, you sure got here in time to save our necks."

Chet, who had set to work cutting away Joe's

bonds, did not yet realize the disaster he had averted. Frank, by now, had pulled out his own knife, and freed Amos Wandy. The old man sat up with a groan, shaking from the recent ordeal.

"Thank heaven!" he said fervently. "Your friend is indeed a lifesaver!"

Joe rose from his chair and yanked the cloth from his mouth. "Chet!" he pounded his pal on the back. "If we said thanks a million times, it wouldn't be enough. Whew! That was the closest squeak we ever had!"

Heaving a deep sigh of gratitude, he asked, "How'd you know we were here, partner?"

"Well," the chunky boy said, "since I hadn't heard from you fellows by late afternoon, I went to your house right after supper. Aunt Gertrude was real worried—said you hadn't come home to eat. I waited with her until after midnight. Then she called the police. All of a sudden, I had a funny feeling you were here, and in trouble, and thought I'd better come pronto to see what was up. So I did."

"And are we glad you had that funny feeling," Frank pointed. "See that black thing? It's a time bomb. If you'd been a minute later, we'd all have been blown to bits."

Chet's ruddy face went white. He stared at the bomb, goggle-eyed.

"Oh—*oh!*" he squeaked, leaping backward as

though fearful it would go off. "Let's get out of here! Quickly! Miles away!"

"I'm inclined to agree," said Amos Wandy wryly, slowly getting to his feet. "But first I must retrieve my invention."

Frank rushed to assist him. "Are you all right, Mr. Wandy? Jensen gave you a hard knock before he tied you up."

"Don't worry about me, young man. I'm just glad you two boys weren't—were saved!" The elderly man looked troubled. "To think, it really would have been my fault—I constructed that terrible bomb."

"But you didn't realize what it was for—that those crooks would use it on people who got in their way, and would destroy this house and all the evidence of what they'd done," Joe assured him solemnly.

"Hey, you detectives," Chet broke in. "About time you filled *me* in on the latest doings in this zany place."

"We will. But first we'd better take cover. Dollars to dimes Jensen'll be back when he realizes the bomb didn't go off. Remember," Frank added, "the police have his car—so he has no means of escape except on foot."

Joe nodded. "That low-down guy's really out of his mind, too. He may come back armed."

Chet looked worried. "Where do we hide?"

For answer, Frank pointed to the secret room behind the clock. Chet, noticing the open wall section for the first time, gaped in astonishment. "Whoever thought of that?"

Amos Wandy turned off the overhead light, and the boys clicked on their flashlights. Then the old inventor led the way into the concealed room. Joe, who was last, clicked off the living-room light, then pulled the wall section after him, leaving it open a crack.

The boys glanced around the room. It was fairly large and well ventilated with air ducts. The Hardys figured it was directly under the secret chamber on the second floor. Their flashlight beams shone on a few pieces of furniture, a workbench, some tools, a hot plate, and a tiny refrigerator.

"All the comforts of home," Joe quipped.

"It did make a fairly good lab," Mr. Wandy recalled wistfully.

As the group crouched in waiting at the door, the Hardys gave Chet a rapid account of the evening's adventure.

"*Ee*-yow!" their friend whistled in a stage whisper. "I hope Mr. Dalrymple appreciates all the necks that have been risked on his case."

Again the Hardys pondered the possible whereabouts of the banker. But they dared not search the mansion for him at present. Eventually the four became silent as they kept their vigil.

The thunder and lightning had diminished. Through the darkness came the familiar *tick-tock*. *Tick-tock*. But now, to Frank, Joe, and Mr. Wandy, it was no longer a dreaded sound.

Suddenly the four tensed. They had heard the front door being opened stealthily. Footsteps entered the living room, and the light came on. Joe put his eye to the crack.

"Jensen!" he reported softly.

The others crowded behind to peer out as well as they could. The ringleader had stopped short in his tracks and was staring fixedly at the disconnected bomb with its torn wire. Slowly his gaze traveled to the two empty chairs and the cut ropes that had held his captives.

"Shall we jump him?" Joe asked eagerly.

Frank shook his head. "Wait."

All of a sudden Jensen seemed to go into a frenzy. His face was livid with rage as he lifted one of the chairs and smashed it to the floor.

"Escaped!" he shrieked. "How could they—"

Beside himself with anger, the man pulled a revolver from his pocket. Aiming it at the ceiling, he shot repeatedly, until the bullets were expended.

"Good place for 'em!" Joe whispered.

Panting, Jensen looked about him wildly, dropping the pistol to the floor. Then suddenly he laughed. "There's one thing they can't prove— that is, if I destroy the invention!" His voice took on a note of cunning. "Amos Wandy—I'll smash his precious invention. Smash it to bits." With that the man wheeled, dashed out of the room, and raced up the stairs.

"No!" gasped Mr. Wandy. "I won't let him do it. I must stop him."

"We all will. Come on!" Frank gave the signal and the four quickly emerged from their hiding place. They raced into the front hall. From the dark stair well they heard Jensen's voice bellowing:

"Those snoopers! They've ruined everything. I'll show 'em. Can't get the best of me that easy!"

The four pursuers ascended the steps, with Amos Wandy in the lead. So eager was the elderly man to rescue his invention that he even outdistanced the boys.

"Mr. Wandy! Be careful!" called Joe in warning.

"I—I must stop that scoundrel!" returned the inventor, "before he reaches the roof."

On the third-floor landing he had to pause for breath. The boys soon caught up to him. Above stretched the flight of stairs leading to the attic.

Frank aimed his flashlight upward into the inky blackness. Its beam revealed Arthur Jensen standing at the top, his back to them.

"Okay, Jensen. You're outnumbered. Get down here and make it snappy!" Frank shouted.

Their enemy jerked around. For a split second the man looked at them almost incredulously.

"Come on, Jensen!" snapped Joe. "You're finished!"

Unexpectedly, the big man plunged down the stairway toward them. He came at such terrific speed that the sheer force of his weight and descent knocked them all down. He landed on top of the heap, grabbed the banister, got up, and pounded down the steps.

"We mustn't let him get away!" Frank yelled. "Chet, you and I will go after him. Joe, you rescue Mr. Wandy. He's heading for the roof! We can't let him climb out there! He's in no condition to do that!"

The boys scrambled apart, and went in two directions. When Joe reached the attic it was empty. But a damp breeze blew in from an open window. He rushed over and peered out.

The rain was still falling steadily, and a cold wind had sprung up. Flickers of distant lightning cast a pale light across the sky.

"Jeepers!" Joe thought. "The poor old man must be out there already. It's very slippery, too!"

The open window faced the ridge of one of the steep slate roofs. In the faint light, halfway out along the ridge, Joe saw a brick chimney.

"Mr. Wandy!" Joe gasped.

Clinging to the chimney with one arm was the drenched, gaunt figure of Amos Wandy. Feet upon the sharp ridge, the old man stood in the chill wind and pelting rain, his free hand reaching for something.

"He might fall!" the boy thought. "I must save him!"

Joe did not wait. He stepped out onto the rain-soaked ridge. Balancing himself carefully, he trod as swiftly as he dared toward the inventor.

"Mr. Wandy!" he shouted. "Wait! I'll help you. Don't move."

The elderly man looked up. "All right. I—I guess I can't get it now."

Finally, Joe was at Amos Wandy's side, "Easy," he cautioned. "Hang on to me. We'll go back slowly."

No sooner had the pair turned away from the chimney, than a powerful gust of wind struck the ridge, catching the inventor off guard. He lost his footing and fell, pulling Joe with him.

Man and boy went tumbling down the slick slate surface toward the edge of the high roof!

CHAPTER XIX

A Narrow Escape

FRANK and Chet had raced pell-mell after Jensen in his flight from the old Purdy mansion. Once outside, the boys trained their flashlight beams in every direction. But the fugitive had already been swallowed up in the darkness beyond.

Chet sighed. "Looks as if Jensen had enough headway to give us the slip," he said in disgust.

Frank nodded. "Afraid so. His bulldozer charge at us gave him a break."

Nevertheless, the boys ran over the grounds, aiming their lights rapidly at trees and shrubbery. But everything appeared serene and quiet in the slackening rain.

Suddenly there came the sound of an automobile roaring full speed up the driveway. With a screech of tires it came to a halt, its headlights on high, in front of the house.

"Police!" Chet cried as six officers leaped from the car and came toward them.

Leading the squad was Bayport Police Chief Collig. "Am I glad to see you!" he exclaimed when he spotted the boys. "We started out as soon as I could get enough men together. Your Aunt Gertrude—"

Frank broke in hastily. "I know. Chet told me she's mighty worried. But we were—er—slightly delayed."

Quickly he related what had taken place that evening to the astonished and horrified chief. "Now," Frank concluded, "I'm convinced Jensen's still on the grounds, hiding. We've had our flashlights on continuously. And if he saw you come in, he probably won't dare try escaping right away."

Chief Collig instantly barked orders to his assistants to begin a hunt for the gang leader. "Search the area all around the house. Just to be sure he hasn't sneaked back inside," he went on, "you, Callahan, turn on every light in the place and scour it from top to bottom."

"Be on the lookout for Mr. Dalrymple," Frank urged, explaining his fears about the banker.

Chief Collig had reassuring news. "Don't worry about him. He telephoned us just before we left. He'd been out of town all day, and called your home. Your aunt told him that you boys were missing. Dalrymple probably will show up here."

By this time the big house was ablaze with lights. The police chief moved off to direct his search detail. Suddenly Frank noted an expression of terror on Chet's face. The stout boy pointed wordlessly toward the roof of the house. Frank turned and froze.

Two figures, swaying back and forth, were hanging onto the edge of the mansion roof.

"Joe! Mr. Wandy!" Frank cried, noting that Joe had one arm around Amos Wandy, and, with his other, was clinging to the gutter.

In a twinkling he was inside the house and taking the steps to the attic two at a time. Chet pounded close behind him.

"If they can only hang on!" Frank thought.

Finally the two boys reached the attic window. "I'll go down for 'em. You straddle the ridge and grab my ankles," Frank directed Chet tersely.

"Got you."

They clambered out onto the rain-slick slates. A dank mist had settled down. Frank crept along the ridge to a spot which he judged to be just above where his brother and Amos Wandy were clinging to the gutter. Chet, directly in back of him, anchored himself on the peak by clamping his legs and heels against either side of the roof.

"Here goes!" Frank maneuvered himself into position, headfirst, on the steep slope. Now Chet grasped his friend's ankles and Frank began his downward slide.

"Joe!" he shouted. "I'm coming after you. Hold on!"

Frank's eyes strained against the blurry mist. Fortunately, the glow from the house lights enabled him to see a little distance ahead. With Chet maintaining an iron grip, Frank Hardy stretched his body full length and reached out toward his brother. He could dimly discern the hands of the dangling pair clutching the roof edge.

But, with a stab of despair, Frank found them inches beyond his grasp. "Chet!" he called. "I—I can't make it."

Above, the chunky boy shifted his position so that he could lean to one side. This gave Frank the needed leeway. Now he slid forward and secured a hold on his brother's hand.

"Joe!" he gasped. "Grab my wrist. See if you can hoist Mr. Wandy up."

He felt Joe's fingers groping, then encircling his lower arm. Joe placed his other hand on the elderly man's elbow and pushed while Frank pulled him by the arm. Slowly and painfully the inventor was dragged up and over the eaves.

Then Joe, with Amos helping despite his weakened state, was hauled back onto the roof. Chet's powerful hold never once failed. For a minute all four remained motionless, catching their breaths.

Then the arduous ascent began. A sort of human chain was formed. Joe held onto Frank's arm, and the inventor onto Joe's ankle. Each had a hand and foot free to help ease the strain on Chet, as they hoisted themselves.

Another inch, and another. Six inches—a foot. At last Frank sat on the ridge beside Chet. A moment later Joe had hooked one leg over the top, and all three assisted Mr. Wandy until he too was astride the peak.

Utterly exhausted, they were silent for several minutes, breathing deeply of the damp air. Finally Joe managed to gasp:

"Guess we put on a real circus act. Trapeze artists have nothing on us."

Mr. Wandy groaned. "I've brought you boys nothing but trouble. I never should have come back here."

"None of us should have come here—ever," was Chet's emphatic comment.

"Just be thankful we're still in one piece," Frank put in dryly. "Let's get going. Collig and his men are below, searching for Jensen—he got away from Chet and me."

Fortunately, the wind had died away, so the trip across the ridge to the attic window was not so hazardous. In vast relief, each of the four clambered back inside.

Mr. Wandy turned to the boys. "I can't thank you enough for all you've done to help me—at your own peril."

"And don't think *I'm* not grateful you two got

to us when you did," Joe told Frank and Chet. "I thought Mr. Wandy and I were on our way down —and out."

Frank smiled at Chet. "Remind me to remind you to keep on eating sirloin steak! You've got arm muscles, pal!"

"You'll buy me a steak after tonight," the stout boy retorted. "Especially if we're going to tangle with loony Jensen again."

The boys started down. As they did, Joe saw Mr. Wandy give a wistful backward glance over his shoulder. Joe suddenly realized that the old man had not yet recovered his invention. In their narrow escape on the roof, the boys had completely forgotten it.

"He doesn't want to bother us again," thought Joe with a pang of pity.

Before anyone could object, he dashed back into the attic, and soon was out on the roof. Back across the ridge he went, straight to the chimney. He felt around it, as Mr. Wandy had done.

Finally Joe's fingers touched a coil of wire with some kind of contraption at the end. Quickly the young detective slipped them into his pocket. Then he hustled back through the window. The others waited for him with perplexed looks.

"Say, haven't you had enough roof travel for one night?" demanded Chet indignantly.

Joe reached into his pocket. "Mr. Wandy—"

The next moment, to the boys' consternation,

the inventor slumped unconscious to the floor.

"We'd better get him downstairs," Frank said worriedly. "He's been through too much."

He and Joe lifted the elderly man and, between them, carried him to the first floor into the living room. Gently they lowered the inventor onto a draped sofa.

Just then Chief Collig strode in, followed by a familiar, straw-hatted figure. "Mr. Dalrymple!" Joe exclaimed.

The banker hurried forward, his face lined and haggard. "Thank heavens you boys are safe!" he cried out. "I'd never have forgiven myself if—"

"We're all right," Frank assured him hastily. "Right now, Mr. Wandy needs help. He fainted."

The police chief instantly summoned one of his men to administer first aid. Briefly, the boys recounted their harrowing experience on the roof. Joe patted his pocket. "I found Mr. Wandy's invention. We'll give it to him later."

Chief Collig, in turn, reported that so far there had been no sign of Arthur Jensen. "I've thrown out a roadblock, too. He's a slippery customer, I must admit."

"To think a would-be murderer was using my property!" Mr. Dalrymple shuddered. "The chief told me everything that happened here. That bomb—awful, awful!"

Assured that Mr. Wandy was rallying satisfactorily, Frank said to Chief Collig, "Okay if we have a try at locating Jensen? I'd like to settle a few scores with him."

"Me too," Joe added grimly.

Chief Collig assented readily. "I can tell you two have a hunch. My men will be on the alert if you need help."

The Hardys and Chet hastened out into the chilly air. The lighted windows of the house became eerie rectangles of hazy yellow in the drifting mist as the trio skirted the dense bushes edging the lawn.

"You figure Jensen eluded the police and circled back to the hidden barn where the gang kept their car?" Joe asked his brother.

"Right," said Frank. "It's worth a look, anyhow."

Chet shivered as they left the lighted house behind and entered the darkness of the road. "Some light would help," he suggested, pulling out his flashlight.

"It would," said Frank in a whisper, "but it might also warn Jensen. We'd better make this trip without lights if we want to take him by surprise."

The three boys stealthily made their way along until they came to the wall of tangled vines where the road ended. Joe pulled aside the vine "curtain." Cautiously they stepped beyond it and moved forward, every sense alert for sound or movement of any kind.

Jensen came toward the boys, lowering the
three-pronged tool threateningly

By now the first faint hint of dawn had light-ened the sky. It made the going easier, but at the same time, the Hardys hoped it would not enable Jensen to spot them.

Shortly the boys reached the big hulk of the ramshackle barn. They stopped to listen. Except for the chirping of crickets, all was silent.

At Frank's signal, the three stepped into the black interior. "We'll have to risk flashlights now," Frank whispered.

Three circles of light stabbed the darkness. The mound of dusty hay was still in the loft above the sagging beam. But most of the camouflaging hay had been thrown aside. The plywood door was open, so the boys peered into the alcove in which the thieves' car had been kept.

A sudden clatter against the wall of the barn caused them to whirl. Chet swung his flashlight swiftly around. Its beam rested on the tall form of Arthur Jensen!

The man's suit was rumpled and soaked. On his face was an expression of mingled rage and hatred. Clutched in his hands was the pitchfork. This was what had caused the clatter—when Jensen had pulled it from its hook.

He came toward the boys, lowering the three-pronged tool threateningly.

"You'll pay for what you've done," the gang leader cried in a voice filled with menace.

CHAPTER XX

Hidden Loot

THINKING quickly, Chet shone his flashlight straight into the eyes of the gang leader as he advanced on the boys with the deadly pitchfork.

Blinded by the glare Jensen stopped.

"Let's separate," Frank whispered. "He can't get all three of us at once!"

The brothers dropped their flashlights and rushed to opposite sides of the old barn. They wheeled and jumped the man from both directions.

Joe came in with a hard-driving tackle that caught Jensen just below the knees. As the man crumpled, Frank stepped in, snatched the murderous pitchfork, and threw it to one side.

Chet had stayed rooted to the spot, keeping his light trained on their would-be attacker. Now he rushed forward, flinging the flashlight away, to help subdue Jensen.

In the darkness a terrific struggle took place. The boys' opponent seemed possessed of an iron strength. Just when they believed they had overpowered him, Jensen would yank loose, flailing his fists violently.

"Don't let him get away!" shouted Frank.

Joe frantically groped in the darkness for the flashlight. He found it and flicked it on. The unexpected beam of light caught Arthur Jensen staggering up the ladder to the haymow. In an instant the boys had pounced on him.

"We'll take no more chances," Frank cried out, whipping off his belt.

Joe quickly unbuckled his also. As Chet held their prisoner in a viselike hold, the Hardys lashed the man's hands firmly behind him with their belts before dragging him out.

The man was sputtering and threatening. "Keep still or we'll gag you!" Frank warned.

Frank and Joe pocketed their flashlights, and the boys marched Jensen along the hidden road back to the house. The old Purdy place was still blazing with lights in the gray dawn. More police cars had arrived, and men were hurrying about in every direction. Chief Collig stood on the front porch directing search operations.

"Good news, Chief!" Frank greeted him as the boys came forward with Jensen.

Collig stared in pleased astonishment. Then he turned to Officer Tomlin, "Call in the men!"

A police whistle shrieked. Immediately the boys were surrounded by officers, two of whom handcuffed Arthur Jensen. The ringleader stood in sullen silence, his eyes burning with hate.

Fleece-lined storm coats were thrown around the chilled boys when the entire group entered the living room. There they saw Mr. Dalrymple looking thoughtfully upon the face of Amos Wandy, who was now sleeping peacefully.

The banker turned to the Hardys. "I thought I recognized Mr. Wandy. I remember him years ago as a brilliant inventor. He came to me once for money to finance an electrical invention of his. I was glad to lend it, knowing that the device would be beneficial to many people. To think he was forced to work on an instrument of destruction by this despicable person."

Mr. Dalrymple gave Jensen a withering look. "But at least," he added, "I'll give Amos any monetary help he may need now, and he can work here any time he wishes, undisturbed!"

The Hardys were pleased to hear this. Joe then said, "We thought something had happened to *you* today, sir. That's what brought us out here tonight."

The banker explained that he had been called out of town on a business emergency early that morning and had no chance to notify his office. "I didn't return until after midnight. When I learned about the Lakeside police having searched my home and why, I contacted your aunt and Chief Collig right away."

The banker addressed the handcuffed Jensen. "How did you—you thugs get into my house?"

"Simple." The gang leader gave a short laugh. "We took wax impressions of the locks, and had keys made in town."

"Yes. But how did you manage to leave threatening notes in my secret room?"

"As I told these snooping kids—find out yourself," was the sullen answer.

Joe had a sudden idea. He drew from his pocket the coil of wire with the mechanism at one end, and examined them for a moment.

The others in the room crowded around. "So this is the invention Amos was keeping on the roof," Frank said, "I wonder why."

The device consisted of a pair of weatherproof batteries mounted side by side on a little platform about three inches long. The platform had wheels, and at one end a pair of little movable jaws.

"If I'm right," Joe observed, "the jaws will open after so many revolutions of the wheels."

He clicked a switch. With a little hum, the metal wheels turned. After a few seconds the jaws opened, and the wheels stopped. When the jaws closed together once more, the wheels turned again—but in the opposite direction!

"Clever," Mr. Dalrymple said. "I think our

government's intelligence department would be interested in this."

"Very clever," Joe replied, "and it's also the method used for delivering those warning notes to your secret room!"

"What!" the banker cried.

Everyone listened intently as Joe explained his theory. "You see, the message was placed in the jaws. Then the whole contrivance was lowered by wire down the chimney. The gadget is small enough to fit through the bars. As soon as it reached the bottom of the fireplace, this platform rolled out into the room and deposited a note! Then it rolled back into the fireplace and was pulled up the chimney by Jensen, on the roof."

Raymond Dalrymple's eyes opened wide in amazement. "No wonder we couldn't figure it out," he declared. "Nobody but myself was entering my secret room!"

Frank wheeled on Jensen. "You convinced Mr. Wandy you wanted to try out his invention. Of course, he didn't know for what purpose."

The prisoner remained stubbornly silent. But Frank's guess was backed up by Amos Wandy himself, who had awakened.

"Mr. Jensen told me he was conducting an experiment," said the inventor. "What a fool I was!"

The captured thief gave a derisive snort. "*That's* true."

"Quiet!" thundered Collig. "You'll have plenty of time to laugh where you're going." The chief signaled two patrolmen, who stepped up to lead Jensen away.

"Wait a moment!" Frank spoke up. "What about the jade? Jensen had it all when he got away from us."

Chief Collig strode over to the gang leader. "Spill it. Where did you stash that jade?"

But no amount of prodding would elicit any reply from Jensen. Finally the chief, in disgust, ordered him to be taken off to jail.

"Looks as if another search operation's in order," Officer Callahan spoke up. "Shall I get the men started, Chief?"

"Right. Also, better douse that disconnected bomb."

"Great jumping Irishmen!" Callahan exclaimed. "I'll say. No use taking any chances!"

Immediately a respectful space was cleared around the formidable black box, and two men carried it outside. Frank, Chet, and Joe followed.

The three boys, although dog-tired, had already determined to conduct their own hunt for the precious jade.

"Where to start?" Chet inquired of his friends.

The Hardys scanned the grounds, still wet from the rain. The sun had risen and was starting to burn off the mist. Frank pointed to a bush area about five hundred yards from the mansion.

"That would've been a good spot for Jensen to hide and watch us get blown up," the boy reasoned.

"Dandy," Joe agreed. "Come on!"

The trio trudged through the wet grass and up the slope. They circled the bushes, and poked among the branches. But there were neither boxes nor a canvas sack. Disappointed, the searchers cast around for another likely place.

Joe's eyes lingered on a huge old maple tree, with low, spreading limbs. "I think I'll climb up," he murmured.

Sprinting to the tree, he swung himself onto the lowest branch. Standing up, he could see the mansion clearly. He then reached out to a stout limb above him and ran his hands along it toward the trunk. His heart leaped as his fingers touched something that felt like canvas!

"Found it!" he shouted.

Frank and Chet dashed up and waited excitedly below. Joe shinned up the trunk. There, tucked in the forked space, was the sack and a pile of small boxes.

"Yippee!" Joe yelled triumphantly. Quickly he lowered the sack and the boxes to his brother and Chet, then jumped to the ground.

Joyfully the Hardys and Chet sped back to Chief Collig. One look at the boys and what they were carrying told him of their success.

"Congratulations!" he said warmly.

"Thanks, Chief," Frank said modestly, then grinned. "We don't like to disappoint clients."

The recovered treasures were taken into police custody. Hurd Applegate's collection and Captain Stroman's jade piece proved to be intact. Their property would be returned to them the following day.

"Oh!" Frank clapped a hand to his head. "I forgot about our stranded car!"

Chief Collig promised to send a tow truck to pick it up. "You fellows had better get some sleep," he advised.

"Swell idea." Chet smothered a huge yawn. "Come on, you detectives! *My* jalopy still runs."

It was seven o'clock that morning when the Hardys wearily entered their home. They had an affectionate reunion with Aunt Gertrude, who had been informed by telephone of their safety.

"Not a word more!" she ordered. "Off to bed! I'll have a good meal ready when you wake up."

Frank and Joe did not argue. They were too tired to be hungry. Soon they were deep in slumber.

The boys were jolted awake in what seemed only a short time by the telephone jangling insistently.

"Oh!" moaned Frank groggily. "Somebody answer the phone!"

But the ringing continued. Joe was still sound asleep. Finally Frank reached out his arm and lifted the receiver of the extension on the night table. "Hello?"

"It will happen while the clock ticks," came a low, menacing voice, "on the dot of six this evening. At the old Purdy place."

"What?" cried Frank, instantly wide awake. "Who is this? Hello! Hello!" The caller had hung up.

"Joe!" he shouted, and shook his brother awake. "Sounds like trouble."

Quickly he told of the sinister phone call. The boys glanced at their clock.

"Good night!" Frank exclaimed. "It's five-fifteen! Almost suppertime!"

Hurriedly the two boys dressed and went downstairs. Aunt Gertrude was not around. They rushed outside to the garage.

"We'll have to use Dad's car," said Joe.

Soon Fenton Hardy's sedan was speeding out Willow River Road. The dashboard clock showed a few minutes before six.

Frank, at the wheel, turned sharply through the open gate and sped up the drive. The old house waited, silent as usual. They went up and tried the front door. To their surprise, it was open!

Cautiously the brothers tiptoed across the empty hall to the closed door of the living room. Frank and Joe paused. *Tick-tock, tick-tock, tick-tock* came the sound of the clock from within.

"Ready?"

"Ready!"

They set their shoulders to the door and burst into the room.

Bong! Bong! Bong! Bong! Bong! Bong! Six o'clock!

"Hooray for the Hardy boys!" came a chorus of voices. "Three cheers for Frank and Joe!"

A crowd of familiar smiling faces confronted the utterly astounded young detectives.

"Aunt Gertrude!" Frank cried out, as his aunt came forward.

"Yes, we're all here." She beamed. "I *told* you there'd be a good meal waiting for you."

She led the way to the dining room. The long table in the center of the room was fully set with glittering glass, china, and silver. Two huge, golden-brown turkeys rested upon oval platters at either end of the table.

At the head sat Raymond Dalrymple. At his right was a happy Amos Wandy. Also present were Chief Collig and Chet Morton, who was grinning from behind one of the turkeys, Hurd Applegate, Captain Stroman, and others of the Hardys' best friends. Among them were Biff Hooper, Tony Prito, Phil Cohen, and Jerry Gilroy. Pretty Iola Morton and Callie Shaw smiled and waved to Frank and Joe.

Speechless with surprise, the brothers were escorted by Aunt Gertrude to chairs beside the girls, then Miss Hardy took her own place.

"All I can say," Joe burst out, "is that this is the best ending to a mystery a fellow could want."

Frank agreed. "There's one more mystery." He grinned. "Who telephoned us today?"

Both boys stared meaningfully at Chet. His suddenly reddening face gave them the answer, and everyone laughed.

"You're not only showing promise as a detective," Frank said with a chuckle, "but you're not a bad actor, either, Chet!"

At this point Mr. Dalrymple, growing serious, stood up. First he read a telegram of congratulation to the boys from Mr. and Mrs. Hardy. Then he said, "I'd like to extend my great appreciation, and that of many others, to the Hardy brothers for helping to rid not only my property, but this whole area, of the harbor thieves. Also, to Chet Morton for his assistance. And all done despite my bad memory about keys. The only one they had was the key they got from the thieves!"

"Hear! Hear!" Captain Stroman and Hurd Applegate led the loud applause.

Mr. Dalrymple continued, "I'd now like to introduce the new permanent resident of this house —Mr. Amos Wandy."

Smiling, he turned to the inventor, who was almost overcome with emotion. Finally, in a trembling voice, Mr. Wandy said, "I can hardly believe my good fortune. A large part of it is due to my three young rescuers."

Amid the excited chatter that ensued, Frank and Joe learned that the banker planned to outfit a regular laboratory for Mr. Wandy. Chief Collig then reported to the boys that Jensen had broken down and given a full confession.

"Was he the rascal who sent me that warning?" Aunt Gertrude demanded.

"Yes, Miss Hardy. But he won't be sending any more threats for a long, long time."

Iola Morton, her eyes dancing, said to the Hardys, "This is one party you won't run out on!"

Callie giggled. "They can't. There's no more mystery."

The boys laughed, and gazed up at the huge clock. Silently, they wondered when another case might come their way. Sooner than they expected, they were to find out, when Frank and Joe spotted strange **FOOTPRINTS UNDER THE WINDOW.**

Mr. Dalrymple rapped for order. "The time has arrived for action. "Do you know what's going to happen—*while the clock ticks?*"

"We eat!" Chet piped up.

Everyone roared with laughter. Then Mr. Dalrymple said, "Hurd Applegate and I are ready to give the Hardy boys their well-earned reward— a fine vacation trip whenever they can take it."

There was loud applause as Frank and Joe stepped up to receive a check made out to the Bayport Travel Agency.